PENGUIN ◉ CLASSICS

THE UNDERDOGS

MARIANO AZUELA (1873–1952), the most prolific novelist of the Mexican Revolution and the author of its most important novel, was born in a small city in the state of Jalisco, Mexico. He studied medicine in Guadalajara and served during the revolution as a doctor with the forces of Pancho Villa, which gave him firsthand exposure to the events and characters that appear in *The Underdogs*. Azuela is buried in the Rotonda de Hombres Ilustres, Mexico's equivalent of Westminster Abbey.

SERGIO WAISMAN has translated Ricardo Piglia's *The Absent City*, for which he received a National Endowment for the Arts Translation Award, and three books for Oxford University Press's Library of Latin America series. He is the author of *Borges and Translation: The Irreverence of the Periphery* and the novel *Leaving*, and is an associate professor of Spanish at The George Washington University.

CARLOS FUENTES is the author of more than twenty books, including *This I Believe, The Death of Artemio Cruz,* and *The Old Gringo*. His many awards include the Rómulo Gallegos Prize, the National Prize in Literature (Mexico's highest literary award), the Cervantes Prize, and the inaugural Latin Civilization Award. He served as Mexico's ambassador to France from 1975 to 1977 and currently divides his time between Mexico City and London.

MARIANO AZUELA

The Underdogs

A NOVEL OF THE MEXICAN REVOLUTION

Translated with an Introduction and Notes by
SERGIO WAISMAN

Foreword by CARLOS FUENTES

PENGUIN BOOKS

PENGUIN BOOKS
Published by the Penguin Group
Penguin Group (USA) Inc., 375 Hudson Street, New York, New York 10014, U.S.A.
Penguin Group (Canada), 90 Eglinton Avenue East, Suite 700, Toronto, Ontario,
Canada M4P 2Y3 (a division of Pearson Penguin Canada Inc.)
Penguin Books Ltd, 80 Strand, London WC2R 0RL, England
Penguin Ireland, 25 St Stephen's Green, Dublin 2, Ireland
(a division of Penguin Books Ltd)
Penguin Group (Australia), 250 Camberwell Road, Camberwell, Victoria 3124,
Australia (a division of Pearson Australia Group Pty Ltd)
Penguin Books India Pvt Ltd, 11 Community Centre, Panchsheel Park,
New Delhi – 110 017, India
Penguin Group (NZ), 67 Apollo Drive, Rosedale, North Shore 0632, New Zealand
(a division of Pearson New Zealand Ltd)
Penguin Books (South Africa) (Pty) Ltd, 24 Sturdee Avenue,
Rosebank, Johannesburg 2196, South Africa

Penguin Books Ltd, Registered Offices: 80 Strand, London WC2R 0RL, England

This translation first published in Penguin Books 2008

5 7 9 10 8 6 4

Translation copyright © Sergio Waisman, 2008
Foreword copyright © Carlos Fuentes, 2008
All rights reserved

Los de abajo published in the United States of America in 1915.

Library of Congress Cataloging in Publication Data

Azuela, Mariano, 1873–1952.
[Los de abajo. English]
The underdogs : a novel of the Mexican revolution / Mariano Azuela ; translated with
notes by Sergio Waisman ; introduction by Carlos Fuentes.
p. cm.
Includes bibliographical references.
ISBN 978-0-14-310527-5
I. Waisman, Sergio Gabriel. II. Title.
PQ7297.A9L613 2008
863'.62—dc22 2008028319

Printed in the United States of America
Set in Adobe Sabon

Contents

Foreword

"Revolutions begin fighting tyranny and end fighting themselves." So said Saint-Just, the French revolutionary who in 1794 was guillotined in the combat between the factions once united against the monarchy. Is this the fate of all revolutionary movements? It does seem to be the case: Russia, China, Cuba. The United States completed its exclusive 1776 revolution and faced Shays' Rebellion only through civil war and battles over civil rights.

The Mexican Revolution (1910–20 in its armed phase) began as a united movement against the three decades of authoritarian rule of General Porfirio Díaz. Its democratic leader, Francisco Madero, came to power in 1911 and was overthrown and murdered in 1913 by the ruthless general Victoriano Huerta, who promptly restored the dictatorship and was opposed by the united forces of Venustiano Carranza, Álvaro Obregón, and Francisco "Pancho" Villa in the north and those of the agrarian leader Emiliano Zapata in the south. But when Huerta, defeated, fled in 1915, the revolution broke up into rival factions. Zapata and Villa came to represent popular forces, agrarian and small town, while Carranza and Obregón were seen as leaders of the rising middle class that Díaz had suffocated under the patrimonialist regime of huge haciendas using low-paid peon labor.

Mariano Azuela (1873–1952) was a country doctor who joined first Carranza, then Villa. In 1915, right in the middle of the war, he sat down and wrote a disenchanted tale of revolution sprung from one man's experience. A chronicle, a novel, a testimony, *The Underdogs* is all of this, but above

all it is a degraded epic, a barefoot *Iliad* sung by men and
women rising from under the weight of history, like insects
from beneath a heavy stone. Moving in circles, blinded by
the sun, without a moral or political compass, they come out
of darkness, abandoning their homes, migrating from hearth
to revolution.

The people of Mexico are "the armies of the night" in
Azuela's book. They give the reader the impression of a violent, spontaneous eruption. But be warned. The immediacy
that Azuela brings to the people is a result of the long medi-
acy of oppression: half a millennium of authoritarian rule by
Aztec, colonial, and republican powers. If this weight of the
past at least partly explains the brutality of the present, it
applies not only to the mass of the people but also to the
protagonists, the leaders, the individuals that Azuela thrusts
forward: the revolutionary general Demetrio Macías and the
revolutionary intellectual "Curro" Cervantes, accompanied
by a host of supporting players. Like the people, Macías and
Cervantes are heirs to a history of authoritarian power and
submission. But if the rebellious mass is moving, however
blindly, *against* the past, Macías and Cervantes are *repeating*
the past. They are rehearsing the role of the Indian, Spanish,
and republican oppressor, Macías on the active front and
Cervantes on the intellectual side. They both see Mexico as
their personal patrimony. They want to be fathers, judges,
teachers, protectors, jailers, and, if need be, executioners of
the people, but always in the name of the people.

The Underdogs thus presents us with a wide view of the
social, political, and historical traits of Mexico and, by ex-
tension, of Latin America: it is a degraded epic but also a
chronicle of political failure and of aspiring nationhood.
There are no Latin American novels prior to independence
in the 1820s. I might say that it is the nation that demands
its narration, but also that narration needs a nation to nar-
rate. This, indeed, links the origins of both the North American and Latin American novel. Whatever they actually are,
they first appeared along with "the birth of the nation."

The novel is a critical event. Religion demands faith, logic

demands reason, politics demands ideology. The novel demands criticism: critique of the world, along with a critique
of itself. While literature and the imagination are deemed superfluous (especially) in satisfied societies, the first thing a
dictatorship does is to censor writing, burn books, and exile,
imprison, or murder writers.

Do we need authoritarian repression to demonstrate the
importance of literature, the critical freedom of words and
the imagination? I cannot separate Azuela's moral and literary significance from the fact that he drew a critical portrait
of the Mexican revolutionary movement as it was happening, setting a standard of critical freedom that has prevailed
in my country in spite of seven decades of authoritarian rule
by a single party. There has been repression in Mexico—of
political parties, individuals, unions, agrarian movements,
journalists—but writers have maintained a high degree of
critical independence. This is thanks to a very early exercise
of this independence by Mariano Azuela and *The Underdogs,* followed by the critical chronicles of Martín Luis
Guzmán, José Vasconcelos, and Rafael Muñoz.

This critical tradition against all odds should be compared
with the silence imposed on Soviet writers by Stalinism, the
exile of German writers from Nazi Germany, or the persecu-
tion of North American authors during the McCarthy era.
The margin of critical and creative freedom, menaced by the
political powers—always, everywhere—was maintained in
Mexico thanks, in great measure, to the stakes planted by
Mariano Azuela.

Azuela began his writing career with a Zolaesque natural-
ist novel, *María Luisa* (1907), and went on to register the
foibles of politics (*Andrés Pérez, maderista,* 1911), political
bosses (*Los caciques,* 1917), the middle classes (*Tribulaciones
de una familia decente,* 1918) and the labor movement (*El
camarada Pantoja,* 1937). *The Underdogs (Los de abajo),*
nevertheless, remains his signature book, and its universal
import is well taken as he describes human conduct that has
the troubling quality of repeating itself everywhere and in all
historical periods. The forces of social ascent and corruption:

"Now we are the swells," the grotesque camp follower *La Pintada* [War Paint] says as she assumes the heritage of the former proprietors.

Corruption unites the best and the worst. In one of the greatest scenes of the novel, several characters, pretending to sleep, see the others in the act of stealing. A common language of dishonesty, cover-up, and government by kleptocracy is born. It is a thieves' pact of worldwide resonance. This is, indeed, a disenchanted epic, in which fatality engenders bitterness and bitterness enhances fatality, both illustrated by the scene where General Macías rolls a stone down a hill, murmuring: "Look at this stone, how it cannot stop."

And yet, perhaps this epic of failures (or failed epic) is a great novel because, for all its realism, even in spite of its cynicism, it is *astonished* by a world it no longer understands. And it is this wonderful sense of surprise that gives *Los de abajo* its lasting wonder.

—CARLOS FUENTES

Introduction

The Underdogs is the most important novel of the Mexican Revolution. In its pages, we follow the actions of a band of revolutionaries—led by the protagonist, Demetrio Macías— at the height of the revolution's armed phase, from 1913 to 1915. The novel works mainly with realism to portray many of the harsh details and effects of the revolution, indirectly drawing our attention to the possible motivations that drive Demetrio Macías and his men to fight. The novel is written in fragmentary prose, and although it is interspersed with moments of beautiful description, it is driven primarily by the dialogue of the protagonists and the surrounding characters themselves. This, combined with frequent, jarring narrative changes—such as alterations in verb tense; choppy, staccato exchanges in the dialogue; and temporal and spatial jumps—serves to reflect the jarring experiences that the characters encounter.

The Underdogs is deeply intertwined with the historical context in which it is set: the Mexican Revolution, and in particular some of the major events of the revolution in the northern states of Mexico. Demetrio Macías and his revolutionary group are followers of the legendary Francisco "Pancho" Villa, the most important revolutionary leader from northern Mexico. The novel begins at the peak of Villa's popularity and ends two years later, when Villa has begun to suffer a series of decisive defeats in the fighting between the different factions of revolutionaries.[1] Part of the route that Macías and his men take in the course of the novel parallels that of another leader of a Villista revolutionary band: Julián

Medina, a historical figure mentioned in passing early on in the novel, who became one of Villa's generals during this time.[2] The relevance here is that Mariano Azuela joined Medina's group and served as its medical officer during almost exactly the same period covered in the novel.[3] The author of *The Underdogs* is thus able to write a novel—Azuela actually began composing the novel while he was with Medina's group—that draws directly on his own experiences of many of the very events that we find when we read the text.

Azuela finished writing the first version of *The Underdogs* in El Paso, Texas, where he took refuge in 1915, and the first edition of the novel was published there.[4] Though it would take nearly ten years—during which time Azuela returned to Mexico and undertook several important rewrites of the novel—and a new publication of the work in Mexico City for *The Underdogs* to begin receiving the kind of critical and popular acclaim it now holds, this cultural connection between Mexico and the United States should not be overlooked. On the one hand, it reminds us of the repeated U.S. involvement in Mexican affairs. On the other, it points to the close, nearly inextricable cultural and social connections that have existed between the two countries at nearly all levels and during almost all moments in modern history. This connection was most certainly present during the Mexican Revolution, and it persisted through much of the twentieth century, remaining very much alive today.

Although they are protagonists in some of the key (and at times bloodiest) events of the Mexican Revolution, the characters of Azuela's novel are in many ways swept up in something they do not quite comprehend. In addition, as Carlos Fuentes points out in his Foreword, if *The Underdogs* can be thought of as an epic—in that it follows Demetrio Macías's travels and battles, from humble beginnings through periods of intense fighting and much glory, and finally back to Macías's original point of departure—then it is certainly a failed epic. I would add that, paradoxically, this constitutes one of the strengths of the novel, as it highlights the fact that *The Underdogs* is replete with ambiguities. Is the novel

revolutionary—in the way it underscores the poverty and ignorance of Mexico's peasants and lower classes, and the in-
justices separating their condition from that of the few
land-owning elite? Or is it counterrevolutionary, in the ways
it reveals the barbarism and banditry of those who fought
on both sides of the revolution, thus suggesting that the objectives of the revolutionaries were personal in nature, as opposed to ideological? Is the novel about the early dreams of
the revolution, or about the eventual and perhaps inevitable
disillusionment with the original objectives of the revolutionary movement? Is the novel meant to be realistic, and is
it trying to chronicle the revolution in a way analogous to
how the printed media and the new technology of the radio
were doing at the time? Or does the novel seek a different
aesthetic altogether, one still rooted in the late nineteenth
century, with its naturalistic and at times *Modernista* de-
scriptions?[5] Or is the novel perhaps already a harbinger of
an avant-garde type of narrative, the first modern Mexican
novel in the line of fiction that Fuentes would famously call
"the new narrative" of Latin America?

Not only is it impossible to resolve these ambiguities, it is
also in fact not desirable to do so. For these ambiguities are
part of what lends *The Underdogs* its importance and its
role as a classic of Latin American fiction. *The Underdogs* is
a foundational text that has helped to shape Mexican identity and Mexican and Latin American literature for nearly a
century, not only influencing subsequent historical novels but
also serving as a model because of some of its narrative tech-
niques. *The Underdogs* forms part of what has come to be
known as the subgenre of the novels of the Mexican Revolution. (The other, most important, early representatives of this
subgenre are Martín Luis Guzmán's 1928 *El águila y la ser-
piente* [*The Eagle and the Serpent*] and Nellie Campobello's
1931 *Cartucho* [Cartucho].) Meanwhile, marks of the influ-
ence of Azuela's *The Underdogs* can be seen in writers from
Juan Rulfo to Carlos Fuentes, to name just two of the most
prominent figures of modern Mexican letters.

The overarching challenge for the translator, then, is to

figure out how to re-create a masterpiece that carries such
weight in its original culture. And the first challenge that the
translator encounters is how to translate the title itself. In
Spanish, *Los de abajo* literally means "those from below."
The novel was translated as *The Underdogs* by E. Munguía
Jr. in 1929, and it immediately became known in English,
and has remained in print, by this title since that date. But
"the underdogs" may not be the best translation of the title.
On the one hand, it has a strong sports resonance that seems
somewhat out of place for such a story. On the other, although Demetrio Macías and his men are unquestionably
those from below—at the most basic level, in an economic
and social sense—it is not clear that the English expression
"the underdogs" captures this same meaning. Macías and
his men are peasants, subjects from the lower classes; they
are in many ways archetypal characters representing the
mostly rural masses who had been excluded from the gains
and benefits of Porfirio Díaz's modernizations, and the very
classes who rose up in the revolution—first against Díaz, then
against Madero, and finally against Huerta (see "Chronology
of the Mexican Revolution," p. xxi).

And yet, "the underdogs" is not entirely an incorrect
translation, either—and besides, as is often the case in literary translation, it is not exactly a matter of "correct" or "incorrect." A better translation may have been "those from
below" or "those from the lower depths," but neither of
these sounds that great, and it would be extremely discon-
certing to English-speaking readers who already know this
novel as *The Underdogs*. In addition, and perhaps most interestingly, although prior to being translated as "the underdogs" this term did not have the same meaning in Spanish as
los de abajo, now that it has been translated as such, it seem-
ingly does have the same—or at least a parallel—meaning.
In other words, translation has not only brought a new
work of literature into our culture, it has also affected our
language. "The underdogs" now means what it has always
meant in English, but it also *connotes* what *los de abajo* de-

notes and connotes in Spanish—at least in the context of the novel in question. For these reasons, Azuela's classic of the Mexican Revolution remains, in my translation in the pages that follow, as *The Underdogs*.

Furthermore, the novel not only has a title that refers to the economic and social condition of its main characters, it also develops a vertical (up/down) metaphor throughout the text that repeatedly plays off of the title. The reader sees this in a number of scenes in which different characters are literally above or below each other—a physical representation meant to reflect or contrast with their economic and social standing. Therefore, I have made every effort, through several details in the translation itself, to re-create the key moments in which the vertical metaphor is operating as a defining subtext of the novel. Similarly, I have sought some new ways, again through specific details of the translation, to make "the underdogs" function as an appropriate title in English.

After the title, the largest challenge the translator faces is that the majority of the novel is written in dialogue, as Azuela has his characters use a variety of regional and colloquial expressions and idioms, and speak in idiosyncratic accents, all of which reflect their different economic and social classes—in addition to their individual personalities. It is crucial that the translator try to re-create at least some of this orality, as it constitutes a defining element of the style. Thus, the manner in which the characters speak is also meant to give the reader a sense of Azuela's characters themselves, and more broadly of the kinds of participants in the Mexican Revolution. In particular, the peasants and the poor in *The Underdogs* are marginal, characters who have not traditionally had a voice—not in history, not in politics, not in literature. The author's careful use of dialogue reflects his intention of having different characters speak for themselves and having the reader hear a variety of voices, some perhaps for the first time. This intention, this oral element of the novel must somehow be re-created by the translator. As the reader will see, I have sought to re-imagine and re-create in English the voices of Azuela's characters, who speak in a very specific kind of Mexican Spanish.

A related challenge for the translator is that most of the characters in the novel are referred to by some sort of nickname, while very few are addressed by their given names. These nicknames—sometimes monikers, other times epithets—often provide the reader a mental image of the characters, of their looks, their personalities, and of how they are seen by those around them. For this reason I have opted, wherever possible within the flow of my version, to render the majority of these nicknames into English. Although translators are usually advised to avoid translating proper names, I believe my decision will give English-speaking readers a more immediate sense of the importance of these nicknames in context. For those interested, each time a nickname first appears in the text, an endnote informs the reader what that nickname was in Spanish. Finally, one nickname simply does not translate well: that of the *curro* Luis Cervantes. In this case, not only is there no direct English equivalent available, but I actually deemed it important to maintain the term *curro*—a derogatory label applied to someone from the upper classes precisely because this individual thinks too highly of himself and looks down with contempt at poor, rural, mestizo, and/or indigenous Mexicans. In addition, as the reader will see, the meaning and the various connotations of *curro* begin to emerge from the text itself, whether one reads the novel in Spanish or in English.

Along these lines, another issue the translator faces is the extent to which certain words should be left in Spanish, perhaps to gain a foreign flavor. In this regard, I have chosen to leave relatively few words in Spanish—and have always provided the definition and my reasoning in the endnote accompanying each such word. On the other hand, I have opted to leave untranslated some words that come from the Spanish but have already been incorporated into English (e.g., "rancho," "señor," "muchacho"). In these cases, I use these specific terms not only because they allow the reader to get a bit closer to the original text, but also because these words are somehow more descriptive, and at times more accurate, than their English equivalents. A good example of this is the word *sombrero*. A sombrero in Spanish is a hat, but within the context of the Mexican Revolution, and of the pages of *The Underdogs*, readers may get a better image of a Mexican character wearing a sombrero—those wide-brimmed palm-leaf hats made famous by Villa and Zapata and their followers during this period—than if they read simply "hat."

As is often the case, the main challenges a translator faces when seeking to bring a literary text from one language and culture (and, in the case of *The Underdogs*, from one historical period) into another are the very elements that make that text important, worthwhile, and pleasurable to read. In other words, it is the very features that make a literary text a classic where a translator encounters the toughest challenges to translating it. It may very well reside in that text's translatability, in the obstacles and challenges to the translation itself, the most prominent of which in *The Underdogs* I have described here. It may also reside in the fact that a defining characteristic of a classic seems to be that it is translated repeatedly through time, as if each new generation required its own new version of that classic, or as if the work itself were constantly calling out for translation. Thus, translation can be said to contribute to the making of a classic—not only by exporting the work into other languages and traditions and by assuring that text's "afterlife," as Walter Benjamin might say, but also by underscoring many of the most fascinating elements of the text, which almost inevitably arise as challenges to the craft of translation. These, then, are some of the central elements that make *The Underdogs* a classic of Mexican—and Latin American—literature. What follows is my attempt to re-create this classic in a new version in English.

—SERGIO WAISMAN

Suggestions for Further Reading

Azuela, Mariano. *Los de abajo: Novela de la Revolucion Mexicana.* Edited with an Introduction, Notes, and Vocabulary by John E. Englekirk. New York, London: Appleton-Century-Crofts, 1939.

Benjamin, Walter. "The Task of the Translator." In *Theories of Translation: An Anthology of Essays from Dryden to Derrida*, edited by Rainer Schulte and John Biguenet, 71–82. Chicago: University of Chicago Press, 1992.

Brenner, Anita. *The Wind That Swept Mexico: The History of the Mexican Revolution of 1910–1942.* With 184 photographs assembled by George R. Leighton. Austin: University of Texas Press, 2003.

Campobello, Nellie. *Cartucho; and My mother's hands.* Translated by Doris Meyer and Irene Matthews. Introduction by Elena Poniatowska. Austin: University of Texas Press, 1988.

Fuentes, Carlos. *La nueva novela hispanoamericana.* México: J. Mortiz, 1969.

Gonzales, Michael J. *The Mexican Revolution 1910–1940.* Albuquerque: University of New Mexico Press, 2002.

Guzmán, Martín Luis. *The Eagle and the Serpent.* Translated by Harriet de Onis. With an Introduction by Federico de Onis. Garden City, NY: Dolphin Books, 1965.

Hernández Chávez, Alicia. Translated by Andy Klatt. *Mexico: A Brief History.* Berkeley: University of California Press, 2006.

Knight, Alan. *The Mexican Revolution.* 2 vols. Cambridge: Cambridge University Press, 1986.

Krauze, Enrique. *Mexico, Biography of Power: A History of Modern Mexico, 1810–1996*. Translated by Hank Heifetz. New York: HarperCollins, 1997.

Leal, Luis. *Mariano Azuela*. New York: Twayne Publishers, 1971.

MacLachlan, Colin M., and William H. Beezley. *El gran pueblo: A History of Greater Mexico*. 2nd ed. Upper Saddle River, NJ: Simon & Schuster, 1999.

Robe, Stanley L. *Azuela and the Mexican Underdogs*. Berkeley: University of California Press, 1979.

Chronology of the Mexican Revolution

1876–80; 1884–1911: Authoritarian rule of Porfirio Díaz, a period known as the Porfiriato. Although Díaz remains in power through presidential elections, he runs unopposed in repeatedly rigged elections, in essence reelecting himself seven times. Díaz undertakes a number of important modernization and liberalization projects in Mexico, but these almost exclusively benefit only the upper classes and the wealthy landowners, creating an ever-increasing gap between rich and poor, between the upper and lower classes, and between cities and rural areas.

November 20, 1910: Francisco Madero issues the Plan de San Luis Potosí, declaring Díaz's regime illegal and calling for a revolution against him. Uprisings erupt primarily in the northern and the southern states of the country.

April–May, 1911: Battle of Ciudad Juárez, in which Pascual Orozco and Francisco "Pancho" Villa defeat the Federale army. Crucial to Madero's overthrow of the Díaz regime.

1911: Díaz goes into exile on May 25. Madero—promising agrarian and land reforms—is elected as the new president with the support of popular leaders such as Villa (from the north) and Emiliano Zapata (from the south), and with an overwhelming majority.

1911–13: Madero's presidency, which had begun as a united effort against Díaz and the Porfiriato, quickly weakens. Madero's refusal to enact agrarian and land reforms causes leaders such as Villa and Zapata to turn against him.

February 9–22, 1913: Victoriano Huerta stages a military coup against Madero in a series of events known as *La decena trágica* (the tragic ten days), which culminate with Madero and his vice president, Pino Suárez, being murdered, and with Huerta taking over as president and establishing a new dictatorship.

Late February 1913: Villa, Zapata, Venustiano Carranza (an early supporter of Madero's efforts to overthrow Díaz), and Álvaro Obregón (who had also contributed in the overthrow of Díaz) join in resistance against Huerta's dictatorship, as they begin fighting against Huerta's army.

October 2, 1913: Villa's Northern Division captures Torreón (in the state of Coahuila). Villa becomes a civil governor for the first time.

December 8, 1913: The Battle of Chihuahua (the capital of the state of Chihuahua). The city of Chihuahua falls to Villa and his Northern Division.

July 1914: After repeated defeats, and given that the United States Navy had seized the seaport of Veracruz to keep Huerta from receiving German arms, Huerta goes into exile. At this point, Carranza takes over as commander in chief of the revolutionary forces.

November 1914: The group of revolutionary leaders who have just defeated Huerta—most prominently Villa, Zapata, Obregón, and Carranza—hold a meeting, known as the *Convención de Aguascalientes* (Aguascalientes Convention), to see if they can settle their differences. However, a rift develops between Villa and Zapata on one side and Carranza and Obregón (i.e., the Constitutionalists) on the other. This leads to intense fighting (often referred to as a civil war) between the various factions.

April 1915: Villa is defeated in the Battle of Celaya by Obregón. Carranza and the Constitutionalists will continue winning most battles and come to control the majority of the country.

May 1915–May 1920: Carranza serves as president, during which time he calls for a constitutional convention. Carranza is the first president under the Mexican Constitution of 1917. Carranza continues successfully fighting off the forces of Villa and Zapata.

May 21, 1920: Carranza is assassinated.

1920–1924: Obregón serves as president.

July 1920: Villa comes to terms with Obregón and retires.

July 20, 1923: Villa is assassinated, shot to death as he was driving his own car in Parral, Chihuahua. The conspirators included Obregón and other of his enemies who feared his return to politics.

Chronology of Mariano Azuela's Life and Work

January 1, 1873: Born in Lagos de Moreno, in the state of Jalisco.

1892–1899: Studies medicine at the University of Guadalajara. Also publishes his first literary short texts during this time.

1907: Publishes first novel, *María Luisa*.

1908–1912: Publishes four more novels.

1911: After Madero's overthrow of Díaz, briefly holds a political position in Lagos. Is an enthusiastic supporter of Madero's early revolutionary goals and presidency.

1913: After Madero is assassinated, joins the resistance against Huerta's forces.

October 1914: Joins the army of Julián Medina, one of Villa's generals, as his medical officer. Travels with Medina's band during their battles; begins writing what would become the text for *The Underdogs*.

April–October 1915: When Villa is defeated by Obregón (in the Battle of Celaya), Medina withdraws to Lagos; Azuela tends to the wounded. Still pursued by Carranza's forces, Azuela flees with a group to Tepatlitán and then Cuquío. Attacked in the canyons of Juchipila, the group Azuela is in withdraws to Aguascalientes and then Chihuahua. The advance of Carranza's troops forces Azuela to flee to Ciudad Juárez and then to take refuge across the border, in El Paso, Texas.

October–November 1915: Finishes composing *The Underdogs* and publishes it in serialized installments in the newspaper *El Paso del Norte*.

December 1915: *The Underdogs* is published in the United States by the very small Paso del Norte press. The novel goes almost entirely unnoticed.

1916: Returns to Guadalajara. Moves with his family to Mexico City. Resumes medical practice and begins a prolific writing career.

1920: After introducing numerous changes and rewrites, Azuela publishes another small edition of *The Underdogs,* this time in Mexico City. Once again, it goes mostly unnoticed by readers and critics.

1924–25: With the fighting of the revolution ended, *The Underdogs* finally starts receiving critical and public recognition and acclaim, and is touted—in Mexico and abroad—from this point on as a masterpiece and as one of the most important novels of the Mexican Revolution.

1917–49: Publishes eleven more novels and receives numerous accolades, becoming one of Mexico's best-known and most important novelists of the twentieth century.

March 1, 1952: Dies of heart failure.

1955–58: Three more of his novels are published posthumously.

The Underdogs

PART 1

I

"I'm telling you that's no animal. Listen to how Palomo[1] is barking . . . That must be a man."

The woman stared out into the darkness of the Sierra.

"Who cares, even if they are Federales?"[2] replied a man, sitting on his haunches in a corner and eating, a small pan in his right hand and three tortillas in the other.

But the woman did not answer him. Her senses were concentrated outside their little house.

The sound of hoofs against stony ground was heard nearby, and Palomo started barking with more anger.

"Either way, it'd be good for you to hide, Demetrio."

Indifferent, the man finished eating. Then he grabbed a pitcher, raised it with two hands, and guzzled down the water. Finally he stood up.

"Your rifle is under the bedding," the woman said in a very soft voice.

The small room was lit by a tallow candle. A yoke, a plow, a goad, and other tilling gear were resting in a corner. Ropes holding up an old adobe molding, serving as a bed, hung from the ceiling. A child lay on faded, torn blankets, sleeping.

Demetrio grabbed his cartridge belt, strapped it around

his waist, and picked up his rifle. Tall, robust, with a bright, beardless red face, he wore a coarse cotton shirt and trousers, a wide-brimmed straw sombrero, and leather sandals.

He stepped out slowly, deliberately, disappearing into the impenetrable darkness of the night.

Palomo, enraged, had jumped over the fence of the corral. All of a sudden a shot was heard, and the dog let out a muffled moan and stopped barking altogether.

A few men on horseback appeared, shouting and cursing. Two dismounted while another stayed with the animals.

"Women, come on out here. Bring us somethin' for dinner! Eggs, milk, frijoles, whatever you have, we're starvin'."

"Damned Sierra! The devil's the only one who wouldn't get lost out there!"

"He would get lost, Sergeant, if he was as drunk as you."

One of the men wore galloons on his shoulders, the other red stripes on his sleeves.

"Where are we, little lady? Well, in here all by herself! Is there anyone else in this here house?"

"So what about that light? And that little kid? Little lady, we want to eat, real quicklike! Are ya comin' out or do we make ya come out?"

"You vile men, you've killed my dog! What harm in the world did my poor little Palomo do to you?"

The woman came back dragging her very white, heavy dog behind her, its eyes already glossed over, its body limp.

"Oh my, look at those plump, rosy cheeks, Sergeant! My dear, don't be angry, I swear I'll turn your house into a dovecote as a namesake to your dog.[3] But for God's sake:

> Don't look at me all irate . . .
> Don't be angry no more . . .
> Look at me sweetly,
> Oh, light of my eyes . . .

the officer finished singing in a harsh voice.

"What is this ranchito called, señora?" the sergeant asked.

"Limón," the woman answered hoarsely, without any fear

in her voice, and turned to fan the coals of the fire and to reach for more wood.

"So this is Limón? Land of the famous Demetrio Macías! Didya hear that, Lieutenant? We're in Limón."

"In Limón, huh? Oh well, what do I care! You know, Sergeant, if I'm headin' to hell, may as well go now, since I got me a good horse anyway. But wouldya look at those little rosy cheeks on that brunette! Tha's the most perfect pair of ripe red apples to bite right into I've ever seen . . ."

"You must know that bandit Macías, señora. I was in the penitentiary with 'im in Escobedo."[4]

"Sergeant, bring me a bottle of tequila. I've decided to spend the night in the kind company of this little brunette here. The colonel? What, why in the world are you speakin' to me about the colonel at these hours? He can go straight to hell as far as I'm concerned! And if he gets upset, as far as I care . . . pop! Go on, Sergeant, tell the corporal to unsaddle the horses and prepare dinner. I'm stayin' right here. Listen, little darlin', you let my sergeant fry up the eggs and warm up the tortillas, and you come 'ere with me. Look, this little wallet of mine is stuffed with bills just for you. It'll be my pleasure. Just imagine! I'm just a little bit drunk tha's why, and tha's why my voice is a little bit hoarse, too. I left half my gullet in Guadalajara, and I've been spittin' the other half all the way up here! So what can you do? It'll be my pleasure. Sergeant, my bottle, my bottle of tequila. But darlin', you're too far away. Come over 'ere, have a drink. What d'ya mean no? Are you afraid of . . . your husband . . . or whatever he is? If he's hidin' in some hole tell 'im to come out. As far as I care . . . pop! Let me assure you I'm not afraid of no rats."

A white silhouette suddenly filled the dark opening of the doorway.

"Demetrio Macías!" the sergeant exclaimed, aghast, taking several steps back.

The lieutenant got up, speechless, and stood cold and motionless as a statue.

"Kill 'em!" the woman exclaimed, her throat dry.

"Oh, forgive me, my friend! I didn't know. But I respect brave men like you, truly."

Demetrio stood looking at them, an insolent and scornful smile warping his features.

"And not only do I respect 'em, I also love 'em. Here, take the hand of a friend. That's okay, Demetrio Macías, I know why you rebuke me. It's because you don't know me, it's because you see me doin' this damned dog of a job. But what d'ya want, my friend! We're poor, we have large families to keep. Sergeant, let's go. I always respect the house of a brave man, of a real man."

After they disappeared, the woman hugged Demetrio tightly.

"Blessed Virgin of Jalpa![5] What a scare! I thought they had shot you!"

"Go on now to my father's house," Demetrio said.

She tried to stop him. She begged, she cried. But he pushed her aside sweetly and answered in a somber voice:

"I can feel that they'll be back with the whole group."

"Why didn't ya kill 'em?"

"Just wasn't their time yet!"

They went out together, she with the child in her arms.

Once at the door, they walked off in opposite directions.

The moon filled the mountainside with dim, hazy shadows.

At every cliff and at each scrub oak, Demetrio could still see the sorrowful silhouette of a woman with her child in her arms.

After many hours of climbing, he turned around to look back. At the bottom of the canyon, near the river, he saw tall flames rising: his house was ablaze.

II

Everything was still in shadows as Demetrio Macías climbed down toward the bottom of the ravine. He was following a path along the narrow incline of a rough slope, between rocky terrain streaked with enormous cracks on one side and a drop of hundreds of meters, cut as if by a single cleft, on the other.

As he descended with agility and speed, he thought:

"Surely now the Federales will find our trail, and they'll jump on us like dogs. Luckily for us, though, they don't know any of the paths going in or out of the ravine. Unless someone from Moyahua[1] is with them as a guide, because the people from Limón, Santa Rosa, and the other ranchitos from the Sierra are reliable and would never turn us in. The cacique who has me running through these hills is from Moyahua, and he'd be more than pleased to see me strung up from a telegraph pole with my tongue hanging down to here . . ."

He reached the bottom of the ravine as dawn was beginning to break. He lay down between the boulders and fell asleep.

The river rushed along, singing in tiny cascades. The birds were chirping, hidden among the pitahaya cacti,[2] while the monotonous cicadas filled the solitude of the mountain with a sense of mystery.

Demetrio woke up, startled. Then he waded across the river and started up the trail on the other side of the canyon. Like a large red ant he climbed toward the crest, his hands clutching like claws at the crags and cut-off branches, the soles of his feet clutching at the trail's round, smooth stones.

By the time he reached the summit, the sun was bathing the high plains of the Sierra in a lake of gold. Looking down toward the ravine, he could see enormous tapered stones, bristling protuberances like fantastic African heads, pitahaya cacti like the ossified fingers of a colossus, and trees stretching out toward the bottom of the abyss. And among the dry boulders and the parched bushes, the bright San Juan roses dawned like a white offering to the star beginning to spread its golden tendrils from stone to stone.

Demetrio stopped at the summit. Then he reached back

with his right hand, pulled out the horn hanging across his back, brought it to his thick lips, and blew into it three times, his cheeks filling out with air as he did so. Beyond the bordering crest three whistles responded to his signal.

In the distance, from among a conical heaping of reeds and rotten hay, many men came forth, one after the other. They were dark and polished like old bronze statues, their chests and legs bare.

Quickly they came to meet Demetrio.

"They burned my house!" he said in response to their inquisitive looks.

There were curses, threats, insults.

Demetrio let them vent. Then he brought a bottle out from his shirt, took a drink, wiped it with the back of his hand, and passed it to the man next to him. The bottle went around from mouth to mouth and was quickly emptied. The men licked their lips.

"God willin'," Demetrio said, "tomorrow, or perhaps even tonight, we will get another close-up of the Federales. What do you say, muchachos? Ready to show 'em 'round these paths and trails?"

The half-naked men jumped up and down, howling with joy. Then they repeated the insults, the curses, and the threats.

"We don't know how many of 'em there's gonna be," Demetrio stated, scrutinizing the faces around him. "But back in Hostotipaquillo,[3] Julián Medina[4] challenged all the pigs and Federales in town with just half a dozen scraggly men armed with knives sharpened on a metate,[5] and he crushed 'em all."

"And what do Medina's men have that we don't have?" said a massive, robust, bearded man with very dark, thick eyebrows and sweet eyes. "All I know," he added, "is that if tomorrow I don't have me a Mauser rifle, a good cartridge belt, pants, and shoes, then my name's not Anastasio Montañés. Seriously! Look here, Quail,[6] don't tell me you don't believe me? I've been pumped fulla lead half a dozen times already. Ask my compadre Demetrio here if you don't believe me. You know, I'm no more afraid of a little ball of candy than I am of bullets. Don't tell me that ya don't believe me?"

"Long live Anastasio Montañés!" Lard[7] yelled.

"No," Anastasio replied. "Long live our leader Demetrio Macías. And long live God in heaven and long live the Blessed Virgin Mary."

"Long live Demetrio Macías!" they all yelled.

They lit a fire using straw and dry wood, and placed strips of fresh meat on the live coals. Gathered around the fire, sitting back on their haunches, they hungrily smelled the meat as it sizzled and crackled on the embers.

Near them, piled up on the blood-soaked ground, lay the golden hide of a calf, while the rest of the meat hung between two huisache trees,[8] suspended with twine, set to cure in the sun and the air.

"Okay, then," Demetrio said. "As you see, other than my thirty-thirty[9] here, we don't have more than twenty rifles. If there's only a few of 'em, we hit 'em until there's none of 'em left. And if there's a lot of 'em, well then, then we give 'em a good run till they're at least good 'n scared."

He loosened the belt from around his waist, untied one of its knots, and offered its contents to his comrades.

"Salt!" they exclaimed with joy, each taking a pinch with the tips of his fingers.

They ate avidly. When they had had enough, they lay back with their stomachs up to the sun and sang sad, monotonous songs, screeching shrill screams into the sky after each verse.

III

Demetrio Macías's twenty-five men slept amid the weeds of the Sierra until the sound of the horn woke them up. Pancracio was blowing it from one of the mountaintops.

"It's time, muchachos. Look alive!" Anastasio Montañés said, inspecting the springs of his rifle.

But an hour went by without the sound of anything other
than the singing of the cicadas in the grassland and the
croaking of the frogs in the hollows.

The first silhouette of a soldier was finally seen along the
tallest ridge of the trail just as the last beams of moonlight
were fading in the slightly pinkish girdle of dawn. After him
others appeared, followed by another ten, and then by another hundred. But all of them quickly vanished in the shadows. And then, as the splendid sun rose and shone brightly,
the side of the cliff was covered with people: tiny men on
tiny horses.

"Look at 'em, how purty they look!" Pancracio exclaimed. "Come on, muchachos, let's go have us some fun!"

Those small moving pieces alternated between blending
into the thickness of the chaparral and blackening farther
below against the ocher of the crag.

The voices of the leaders and the soldiers could be heard
distinctly below them.

Demetrio gave a signal, and the springs of all the rifles
stretched and cocked.

"Fire!" he ordered in a hushed voice.

Twenty-one men fired at once, and as many Federales fell
from their horses. The others, surprised, remained stationary, like bas-reliefs against the side of the cliff.

A new discharge, and another twenty-one men rolled
from rock to rock, their skulls cracked.

"Show yourselves, bandits! Come out, dirty dogs!"

"Death to the corn-grinding thieves!"

"Death to the cattle rustlers!"

The Federales yelled at the enemy, but Macías and his men
remained hidden, stationary, and quiet, happy simply to continue practicing a marksmanship that was already their pride
and fame.

"Look, Pancracio," said the Indian,[1] a man dark everywhere except for his teeth and the whites of his eyes. "This
bullet's for the one tha's tryin' to run behind that pitahaya
cactus over there! Son of a . . . ! Take that! Didya see that,

right in 'is head? Now for the one ridin' on that gray horse . . . Down you go, you blockhead!"

"I'm gonna give that one who's ridin' along the ridge of the trail there a nice bath. You watch an' tell me if he doesn't fall right in the river, that no-good conservative pig down there. How 'bout that? D'ya see 'im fall right in?"

"Come on, Anastasio, don't be cruel! Let me use your rifle. Come on, let me have just one shot!"

Lard, Quail, and the others who did not have firearms asked to use them, begging to be able to take at least one shot, as if asking for some supreme favor.

"Show yourselves, if you're men enough!"

"Come out, mongrels. You lousy dogs."

The shouts could be heard from one side of the mountain to the other as clearly as if they were coming from across a street.

All of a sudden Quail emerged from his hiding place with his pants off, and waved his trousers to tease the Federales, pretending he was fighting a bull. At that point shots began raining on Demetrio's men.

"Uh-oh! I think they launched a hornet's nest over my head," Anastasio Montañés said, already crouching down and hiding between the stones, not daring to look up.

"Quail, you son of a . . . !" Demetrio roared. "Everyone, now, over to where I said before!"

They dragged themselves along and took up a new position.

The Federales began to shout with joy, celebrating their perceived victory. But just as soon as they had ceased firing, a new hailstorm of bullets baffled them again.

"There's more of 'em here now!" the soldiers clamored.

Overwhelmed and panicked, many turned their horses around and retreated at once, while others abandoned their horses and climbed off, seeking refuge among the boulders. The leaders fired over the heads of the fugitives in an attempt to restore order.

"Get them dogs down below. Get them dogs down be-

low," Demetrio yelled, aiming his thirty-thirty down toward
the crystalline stream of the river.

A Federale fell into those very waters. And without
fail, with each shot Macías took another man fell, one after
the next, into the abyss. But he was the only one shooting
down at the Federales near the river, and for each one that
he killed, ten or twenty climbed unharmed up the other
slope.

"Get them dogs down below. Get them dogs down below," he kept shouting, enraged.

Now sharing their weapons, the comrades were placing
bets as they aimed at and hit their targets.

"My leather belt if I don't hit the one on the spotted gray
horse in the head. Lend me your rifle, Indian."

"Twenty rounds for your Mauser and half a vara[2] of
chorizo if you let me shoot the one ridin' that black mare
with a white mark on its forehead. Ready . . . now! Didya
see how high he jumped? Like a deer!"

"Don't run off, you conservative mongrels! Come meet
your Papi Demetrio Macías."

Now Macías's men were the ones yelling out the insults.
As Pancracio shouted, his smooth, otherwise immutable-as-
stone face became completely distorted. And as Lard roared,
the muscles on his neck tightened and the lines on his face
stretched out, his eyes murderously grim.

Demetrio continued shooting and warning his men of
their grave danger, but they ignored his desperate cries until
they heard the bullets whizzing right over their heads.

"I'm hit, I'm hit!" Demetrio yelled, gnashing his teeth together. "Sons of a . . . !" he exclaimed as he slid down between the boulders of the ravine.

IV

Two men were missing: Serapio the candy maker and Antonio, who played the cymbals in the Juchipila[1] band.

"We'll just have to see if they can catch up with us farther along," Demetrio said.

They were disheartened. Only Anastasio Montañés maintained that sweet expression in his sleepy eyes and bearded face, while Pancracio maintained the repulsive immutability in his hard profile and his protruding jaws.

The Federales had retreated. Demetrio was gathering all the horses that had been left behind, hidden in the Sierra.

All of a sudden Quail shouted from where he was marching out in front: he had just seen the missing comrades, hanging from the branches of a mesquite tree.

It was Serapio and Antonio. When they recognized them, Anastasio Montañés muttered a prayer between his teeth:

"Father who art in heaven, hallowed be thy name . . ."

"Amen," the others murmured, their heads bowed, their hats off, held tightly against their chests.

Afterward, they immediately set off along Juchipila canyon, heading north, without taking any rest at all, even though it was already well past nightfall.

Quail did not leave Anastasio's side for a single moment. The silhouettes of men hanging and swaying softly in the breeze—necks limp, arms drooping, legs rigid—would not fade from his memory.

The next day Demetrio began to complain heavily about his wound. He could no longer ride his horse. To be able to continue from there they had to improvise a stretcher out of oak branches and bundles of grass.

"You're still bleeding, compadre Demetrio," Anastasio Montañés said. So he tore off one of the sleeves from his shirt, ripped a long strip from it, and tied it firmly around Demetrio's thigh, just above the bullet wound.

"Okay," Venancio said. "That'll stop the bleeding and ease the pain."

Venancio was a barber, and in his town he pulled molars and applied caustics and leeches. To a certain extent, the men looked up to him because he had read The Wandering Jew and The Sun of May.[2] He was a man of few words who was

well satisfied with his own wisdom, and whom everyone
called doctor.

They took turns carrying the stretcher, four at a time,
through barren, rocky mesetas and along very steep slopes.

At noon, when the heat was stifling and a low-lying haze
made sight uncertain, the only sounds to be heard were the
measured, monotone complaints of the wounded man accompanied by the incessant singing of the cicadas.

They stopped and took their rest at every small hut they
found along the way, always tucked into the craggy boulders
of the Sierra.

"Thank God that there's always a compassionate soul
waitin' with a big ol' bowl of chilies and frijoles!" Anastasio
Montañés said, burping.

And very enthusiastically shaking the calloused hands of
Demetrio Macías's men, the men from the Sierra would exclaim:

"God bless you! God help you and lead you along the
road! Today you're heading out. Tomorrow, we'll run too,
running from the draft, chased by those damned government criminals who have declared a war to the death on all
us poor people. You know that they steal our pigs, our
chickens, and even the little bit of corn that we have to eat.
You know that they burn our houses and take our women.
And then, wherever they track you down, right there and
then they finish you off as if you was a rotten dog."

As the sun set in a sudden blaze that imbued the sky with
bright, vivid colors, they saw up ahead a handful of small,
drab houses huddled together in a clearing between the
bluish mountains. Demetrio had his men take him there.

They found a few very poor straw huts at the river's edge,
surrounded by newly sprouted corn and frijole seedlings.

They set the stretcher down on the ground; Demetrio
called out in a weak voice, asking for a drink of water.

Faded skirts, bony chests, and disheveled heads gathered
in the dark mouths of the humble dwellings, while bright
eyes and ruddy cheeks stayed congregated inside.

A chubby little boy with shiny dark skin went up to see

the man on the stretcher. He was followed by an old woman, and then everyone else came out and surrounded Demetrio.

A very friendly girl brought a jícara[3] filled with blue water. Demetrio grabbed the gourd with his trembling hands and drank avidly.

"Want any more?"

Demetrio raised his eyes: the young woman had a very ordinary face, but her voice was filled with much sweetness.

He wiped the sweat spotting his forehead with the back of his fist, turned over to one side, and uttered weakly:

"May God bless you for this!"

Then he began to shiver so strongly that the grass bed and the legs of the stretcher started to shake as well. The fever finally made him lethargic.

"It's gettin' damp out and tha's bad for the fever," said Señora Remigia, a barefoot, hunched-over old woman wearing a coarse cotton rag across her chest as a shirt. She invited the men to bring Demetrio into her hut.

Pancracio, Anastasio Montañés, and Quail lay down at the foot of the stretcher like loyal dogs, attentive to anything their leader might need.

The others headed out in search of food.

Señora Remigia offered them what she had: chilies and tortillas.

"Just imagine! Not long ago I had eggs, chickens, there was even a baby goat that was born here. But these damned Federales cleaned me out."

Later, cupping her hands around her mouth, she whispered into Anastasio's ear:

"Just imagine! They even took Señora Nieves's youngest daughter!"

V

Quail opened his eyes and sat up, startled:

"Montañés, didya hear that? A gunshot! Montañés . . . wake up!"

Quail pushed Montañés hard several times, until he got him to move and stop snoring.

"Son of a . . . ! You botherin' me again? I tell ya that the dead don't come back to haunt us . . ." Anastasio muttered, half awake.

"I heard a gunshot! Montañés!"

"Go to sleep, Quail, or you're gonna get it . . ."

"No, Anastasio. I'm tellin' ya this is no nightmare. I've stopped thinkin' about those men that was hung. I really heard a gunshot. I heard it nice and clear."

"So you're sayin' ya heard a gunshot? Let's see, hand me my Mauser."

Anastasio Montañés rubbed his eyes, lazily stretched out his arms and legs, and stood up.

They walked out of the hut. The sky was covered with sparkling stars, and a moon was rising like a thin scythe. The confused rustling of frightened women could be heard inside the small houses, as well as the sound of men who had been sleeping outside and were also waking now and grabbing their weapons.

"You idiot! You've broken my foot!"

The voice was heard clearly and distinctly nearby.

"Who goes there?"

The sound echoed from boulder to boulder, from hill crest to hill dale, until it was lost in the distance and silence of the night.

"Who goes there?" Anastasio repeated in a louder voice, cocking the bolt of his Mauser.

"I'm with Demetrio Macías!" the answer came from close by.

"It's Pancracio!" Quail said, relieved. Then, no longer concerned, he rested the butt of his rifle on the ground.

Pancracio was leading a young fellow covered entirely in dirt, from his American felt hat down to his worn-out, clumsy shoes. He had a fresh stain of blood on one of the legs of his trousers, near his foot.

"Who's this *curro*?"[1] Anastasio asked.

"There I am, keeping guard, when I hears a sound in the

bushes, so I shout: 'Who goes there?' And this guy answers: 'Carranzo.'[2] So I think, 'Carranzo, I don't know no bird with no name like that.' So I say, here goes your Carranzo, and I filled one of his legs with lead."

Pancracio smiled and looked around with his beardless face, waiting for his applause.

At that point the unknown man spoke:

"Who is the leader here?"

Anastasio raised his head proudly, facing him.

The young man lowered his voice a bit.

"Well, I too am a revolutionary. The Federales grabbed me in one of their levies, and I joined their files. But in the battle the day before yesterday I was able to desert, and I have come, on foot, looking for your group."

"Oh, he's a Federale!" said a number of men in response, looking at him with wonder.

"Oh, he's one of those conservative mongrels!" Anastasio Montañés said. "Why didn't you pump his head full of lead instead of his foot?"

"Who knows what he's up to. Says he wants to speak to Demetrio, that he's got God knows what to tell 'im. But before he does anythin' like that, there's plenty a' time for us to be doin' whatever we wanna with 'im," Pancracio said, raising his rifle and aiming it at the prisoner.

"What kind of animals are you?" the unknown man demanded.

But he was unable to say anything further because Anastasio slapped him across the face with the back of his hand, snapping the prisoner's now-blood-drenched head backward.

"Kill the damned mongrel!"

"Hang 'im!"

"Burn the Federale alive!"

Shouting and howling and all worked up, they started to ready their rifles.

"Hush, hush. Quiet now! I think Demetrio is talking," Anastasio said, urging them to calm down.

Demetrio did as a matter of fact want to find out what was going on, so he had the prisoner brought to him.

"It's a disgrace, dear leader, just look. Look!" Luis Cervantes exclaimed, showing Demetrio the blood on his pants and his swollen mouth and nose.

"Enough, enough. For God's sakes then, just tell me, who are you?" Demetrio demanded.

"My name is Luis Cervantes. I am a medical student and a journalist. I was pursued, trapped, and made a prisoner—all for having said something in favor of the revolutionaries."

The story that he proceeded to tell of his most recent adventure, in his bombastic style, made Pancracio and Lard double over with laughter.

"I have sought to make myself understood, to convince your men here that I am truly a coreligionist."

"A co-re a . . . what?" Demetrio inquired, perking up his ears.

"A coreligionist, dear leader, which is to say, that I am a believer of the same ideals and that I fight for the same cause as you and your men."

Demetrio smiled.

"Well, tell me, then: what cause exactly are we fighting for?"

Disconcerted, Luis Cervantes did not know how to answer.

"Look at 'im, look at that expression on his face! Why make 'im jump through so many hurdles? Can't we go ahead and shoot 'im dead now, Demetrio?" Pancracio asked anxiously.

Demetrio brought his hand up to the tuft of hair covering one of his ears and scratched for a long while as he considered the situation. Then, unable to find a satisfactory solution, he said:

"Get outta here, everyone. My wound's startin' to hurt again. Anastasio, blow out that flame. And lock this one up in the corral. And Pancracio and Lard, you watch over 'im. We'll decide what to do with 'im tomorrow."

VI

Still unable to discern the specific shapes of the objects around him by the dim light of the starry nights, Luis Cervantes searched about for the best place to rest. Eventually he brought his exhausted bones to a pile of wet manure and laid his long body down under the broad canopy of a huisache tree. More out of sheer fatigue than resignation, he forced himself to close his eyes, determined to sleep until his fierce guards woke him up, or until the morning sun burned his head—whichever came first. But he felt some kind of vague warmth next to him, followed by a coarse and labored breathing, and he began to tremble. He reached his shaking hand out and touched the bristling hairs of a pig. The animal, in all likelihood annoyed by the man's proximity, began to grunt.

All of Luis Cervantes's efforts to sleep after that were in vain. Not because of the pain in his wounded limb, nor that which he felt all over his battered and bruised body, but because of the vivid and clear failure he sensed within himself.

Yes. He had not realized early enough how great the distance would be between handling a verbal scalpel—between hurling factious bolts from the columns of a provincial newspaper—and coming out with a rifle in hand to hunt out the bandits in their own den. He was already beginning to suspect his mistake when he was discharged as a cavalry second lieutenant, at the end of the first day. It had been a brutal day in which they had covered fourteen leagues, leaving his hips and knees stiff as a board, as if all his bones had fused into one. He finally understood it eight days later, at the first encounter with the rebels. He could swear upon the Holy Bible itself that when the soldiers had brought their Mausers up to take aim, someone behind him had said in an extremely loud voice: "Every man for himself!" This was so clearly so that his own spirited, noble steed, which was otherwise accustomed to combat, had turned on its hind legs and galloped away, without stopping until they were at a very safe distance from where the firing of the rifles could be heard. By then the sun was already setting, the mountains filling with vague, unsettling shadows, and the darkness was quickly rising from the bottom of the ravines. Was there anything more logical for him to do, then, than to search for shelter among the boulders, and to rest his weary bones and spirit and try to sleep? But a soldier's logic is the logic of the absurd. For the following morning his colonel kicks him awake and drags him out of his hiding place, and proceeds to bash his face in. And there is more yet: the officers find this so deeply hilarious, they are so beside themselves with laughter, that all of them beg that the fugitive be pardoned. So the colonel, instead of sentencing him to be shot by firing squad, gives him a hearty kick on his behind and sends him to take care of the pots and pans as a helper in the kitchen.

This gravest of affronts was to yield its venomous fruits. From then on Luis Cervantes would change uniform, although only *in mente* for the time being. The suffering and the misery of the dispossessed would eventually move him; he is to see their cause as the sublime cause of an oppressed people demanding justice, pure justice. He becomes friends with the humblest of the common soldiers, and one day even comes to shed tears of compassion for a mule that dies at the end of an arduous journey.

Luis Cervantes thus made himself deserving of the good-will of the troop. Some soldiers even dared to confide in him. One, a very serious soldier known for his calm, his moderation, and his reserve, told him: "I'm a carpenter. I had my mother, a little ol' lady who hadn't been able to get up from her chair for the last ten years because of her rheumatism. At midnight three soldiers grabbed me from my house. By the time I woke up, I myself was a soldier in the barracks. Then, by the time I went to sleep that night, I was already twelve leagues away from my hometown. A month ago we go by there with the troop again, and my mother's already six feet under! There was nothin' in this life to console her no more. Now no one needs me. But with God above in the heavens as my witness, I swear that these cartridges that I'm carryin' right here are not gonna be used for the enemies. And if the miracle of miracles is granted to me, if the Most Holy Mother of Guadalupe[1] grants me the miracle, and I am allowed to join Villa,[2] then I swear on my mother's blessed soul that I'll make these Federales pay for it."

Another, a young soldier—very intelligent but a real blabbermouth who was an alcoholic and a marijuana smoker—called him apart, looked straight at him with his hazy, glassy eyes, and whispered into his ear: "Compadre, those men . . . Do you understand what I'm trying to tell you? Those men on the other side . . . Do you understand? They ride the choicest horses from the stables of the north and the interior, the harnesses on their horses are made of pure silver. And us? Pshaw! We ride sardines that can barely pull a pail out of a chain pump. Do you understand what I'm trying to tell you, compadre? Those men, the ones on the other side, they get shiny, heavy gold coins. And us? We get lousy paper money made in the factory of that murderer.[3] What I'm tryin' to say is . . ."

They all went on like this. There was even a second sergeant who ingenuously told him: "It's true, I enlisted, but I really made a mess of it when I chose this side. What in times of peace you'd never make in a lifetime of workin' like a mule, today you can make in just a few months of runnin' through the Sierra with a rifle on your back. But not with these men, brother, not with these men . . ."

And Luis Cervantes, who already shared with the common soldier this concealed, implacable, and mortal hatred toward the upper classes, the officers, and all superiors, felt that the very last strands of a veil were being lifted from his eyes, as he now saw clearly what the outcome of the struggle had to be.

"And yet here I am today. When I finally arrive to join my coreligionists, instead of welcoming me with open arms, they lock me up in a pigsty . . ."

Morning arrived: the roosters crowed in the shacks, while the chickens stirred about on the branches of the huisache trees in the corral, spread their wings out, ruffled their feathers, and jumped straight down to the ground.

Luis Cervantes observed his guards, lying down in the manure, snoring. In his imagination the physiognomies of the two men from the evening before came back to life. One, Pancracio, was light-haired, beardless, with a freckled face, protruding chin, flat, slanted forehead, ears smeared onto his cranium, and all in all he displayed a bestial appearance. The other, Lard, barely looked human, with sunken, grim eyes, thick, always parted reddish lips, and very straight hair that came down to his neck, over his forehead and ears.

Once again Luis Cervantes began to tremble.

VII

Still drowsy, Demetrio ran his hand over the curled tufts of hair covering his wet forehead, pushed it aside toward one of his ears, and opened his eyes.

He heard the melodious feminine voice he had already been hearing distinctly in his dreams, and turned toward the door.

It was daytime: the rays of sunlight darted through the hut's straw roof. The same girl who, the evening before, had offered him a little gourd full of deliciously cold water (his dreams throughout the night), now entered—just as sweet and affectionate—with a pot of milk, its foam spilling over.

"It's goat's milk, and it's more than good. Go on now, try it."

Grateful, Demetrio smiled, sat up, and took the earthenware bowl. He started taking small sips without moving his eyes from the girl.

Restless, she lowered hers.

"What's your name?"

"Camila."

"I'm likin' that name, and even more your sweet little voice."

Camila blushed all over. Then, seeing that he tried to

reach out and grab her wrist, she picked up the empty bowl and very quickly fled the hut, frightened.

"No, compadre Demetrio," Anastasio Montañés remarked seriously. "You have to break 'em in first. H'm. If I was to tell you all the marks that women have left on my body! I've got a lot of experience with all that."

"I feel fine, compadre," Demetrio said, pretending he had not heard him. "I think I got the chills. I sweated a lot and woke up very refreshed. What's still bothering me is the damned wound. Call Venancio so he can cure me."

"So what should we do with that *curro* who I caught last night, then?" Pancracio asked.

"Oh, tha's right! I'd forgotten all about 'im."

Demetrio, as always, thought and hesitated much before making a decision.

"Let's see, Quail, come here. Listen. Find out how to get to a chapel tha's about three leagues from here. Then go and steal the priest's cassock."

"But what are we gonna do, compadre?" Anastasio asked, dumbfounded.

"If this *curro* has come to kill me, it's very easy to get the truth out of 'im. I'll tell 'im that I'm havin' 'im shot to death. Then Quail dresses up like a priest and takes his confession. If he confesses to the sin, I do 'im in. If not, I let 'im go."

"H'm, so much ado! I should've just blasted 'im and finished it right then and there," Pancracio exclaimed contemptuously.

That evening Quail returned with the priest's cassock. Demetrio had the prisoner brought to him.

Luis Cervantes came in. He had not slept or eaten in two days, his face was pale, he had bags under his eyes, and his lips were colorless and parched.

He spoke slowly and awkwardly.

"Do with me what you will. I was probably wrong about you and your men."

There was a drawn-out silence. And then:

"I thought that you would gladly accept someone who

came to offer his help, as small as my help may be to you, and yet of benefit only to you. What do I care, after all, if the revolution succeeds or not?"

As he spoke out loud, he slowly began to regain his confidence, and eventually the languor in his eyes began to fade.

"The revolution benefits the poor, the ignorant. It is for him who has been a slave his entire life, for the wretched who do not even know that they are so because the rich man transforms the blood, sweat, and tears of the poor man into gold—"

"Bah! What're we supposed to do with all of that? I never cared much for sermons!" Pancracio interrupted.

"I wanted to fight the blessed struggle of the poor and the weak. But you do not understand me, you reject me. And so I say: do with me what you will!"

"Well, maybe I'll just put this here rope 'round your throat, which sure is nice 'n chubby 'n white, isn't it now?"

"Yeah, I know what you're here for," Demetrio responded sharply, scratching his head. "I'm havin' you shot to death, eh?"

Then, turning to Anastasio:

"Take 'im away. And if he wants to confess, bring 'im a priest."

Impassive as always, Anastasio gently grabbed Cervantes's arm.

"You're comin' with me, *curro*."

When Quail showed up a few minutes later, dressed in the cassock, they all burst out laughing.

"H'm! This *curro* sure can talk," he remarked. "I think he was even havin' a laugh at me when I started askin' 'im questions."

"But he didn't sing nothin'?"

"Nothin' more than what he said last night."

"I'm thinkin' that he didn't come here to do what you fear, compadre," Anastasio noted.

"Okay then. Give 'im somethin' to eat and keep an eye on 'im."

VIII

The next day, Luis Cervantes could barely get up. Dragging his wounded leg about, he wandered from house to house asking for a little alcohol, some boiling water, and shreds of rags. Camila, with her tireless friendliness, supplied him with everything.

She sat next to him and watched him treat himself, observing with the curiosity typical of someone from the Sierra as he rinsed out the wound.

"Listen, and who taught ya to cure like that? And whatcha boil the water for? And the rags, whatcha sew 'em together for? Well, wouldya look at that. How curious. And what're ya pourin' on your hands? Is that really alcohol? Well, what d'ya know, I thought alcohol was only good for colic! Ah! So ya was gonna be a doctor, really? Ha, ha, ha! What a laugh riot! And wouldn't it be better if ya put some cold water on there? You sure do tell some fantastic stories! Little tiny animals livin' in the water if you don't boil the water! Phooey! I sure don't see nothin' when I look at it!"

Camila continued asking him questions with such a friendly nature that before long she was addressing him informally.[1]

But Luis Cervantes, lost in his own thoughts, was no longer listening to her.

"So where are those admirably armed men and their steeds, those men who are receiving their wages in solid gold coins that Villa is minting in Chihuahua. Bah! All we have here is twenty-some half-naked, louse-ridden men, one of them even riding a decrepit old mare, nearly whipped to death from its withers to its tail. Could it be true, then, what the government press and what he himself had claimed before, that the so-called revolutionaries were nothing more than a bunch of bandits grouped together under a magnificent pretext just to satiate their thirst for gold and blood? Could it be, then, that everything that was said of them by those who sympathized with the revolution was a lie? But if the newspapers were still loudly touting all the many victories of the federation,[2] then why had a paymaster recently arrived from Guadalajara spreading the rumor that Huerta's friends and family were abandoning the capital and heading toward the ports on their way to Europe, even though Huerta kept shouting and yelling, 'I'll make peace, no matter the cost.' So the revolutionaries, or the bandits, or whatever one wished to call them—they were going to topple the government. Tomorrow belonged to them, and the only choice, the only choice really, was to join them.

"No, this time I have not made a mistake," Luis Cervantes said to himself, almost out loud.

"What're ya sayin'?" Camila asked. "I was startin' to think that a cat had gotten your tongue."

Luis Cervantes frowned and looked angrily at the girl, a kind of homely female monkey with bronze-colored skin, ivory teeth, and broad, flat feet.

"Listen, *curro*, ya must know how to tell stories, don't ya now?"

Cervantes made a rude gesture and left without answering her.

Enthralled, she continued looking at him until his silhouette disappeared down the path by the river.

She was so distracted that she nearly jumped, startled, when she heard the voice of her neighbor, the one-eyed María Antonia, who was as always snooping from her hut. María Antonia had shouted at her:

"Hey, you! Give 'im some love powder. Maybe then he might fall for ya."

"Nah. You might, but not me."

"You bet I'd like to! But, phooey! Those *curros* make me sick."

IX

"Señora Remigia, won't you lend me some eggs, my chicken woke up all lazy. I have some señores back there who want breakfast."

The neighbor opened her eyes wide, trying to adjust her sight as she passed from the bright sunlight into the shadows of the small hut, made darker still by the dense smoke rising from the fire. After a few brief moments she could make out the outlines of the objects in the room more distinctly, and she saw the stretcher of the wounded man in a corner, with the man's head close to the dilapidated, greasy posts of the wall.

She crouched down next to Señora Remigia, glanced furtively toward where Demetrio was resting, and asked in a hushed voice:

"How's this man doing? More comfortable, ya say? Tha's good. Look at 'im, he's so young. But he still looks so pale and ghastly. Ah! So the bullet wound won't heal, huh? Listen, Señora Remigia, shouldn't we do some kinda healin' ourselves?"

Señora Remigia, naked from the waist up, stretches her lean, sinewy arms out over the handle of the metate, and presses it down and back and forth over her nixtamal,[1] grinding the corn over and over again.

"Who knows if they'll like that any," she answers without interrupting her tough task, nearly out of breath. "They have their own doctor, ya know."

"Señora Remigia." Another neighbor comes in, bending her bony body down to pass through the door. "Do ya have a few leaves of laurel ya could give me to prepare an infusion for María Antonia? She woke up with the colic."

And since this request was merely a pretext to come in and gossip, she turns her eyes toward the corner where the wounded man is lying, and inquires about his health, winking.

Señora Remigia lowers her eyes to indicate that Demetrio is sleeping.

"Well, so you're here too, Señora Pachita, I hadn't seen ya."

"Good mornin' and God bless you, 'ñora Fortunata. And how's your family this mornin'?"

"Well, María Antonia has got her the 'curse.' And, as always, she's got the colic."[2]

She squats down and crouches right next to Señora Pachita.

"I don't have any laurel leaves, dear," Señora Remigia replies, stopping her grinding for a moment. She wipes a few stray locks of hair that had fallen over her eyes from her drenched face. Then she digs her two hands deep into the earthenware tub and pulls out two large handfuls of cooked corn, dripping a turbid, yellowish water. "I don't have any. You should ask Señora Dolores, though. She's always got all kinds of herbs."

"'ña Dolores left for the convent last night. They came to get 'er without any warning so she'd go help Uncle Matías's girl."

"Go on, Señora Pachita. You don't say!"

The three old women form a lively chorus, gossiping in very low, hushed tones, but always in a very vivid, animated manner.

"As sure as there's a God in heaven above us!"

"Well, ya know, I'm the first one who said anything about it: 'Marcelina's big,' I said, 'she's really big 'round the middle!' But no one wanted to believe me."

"Well, poor thing. And what if the baby turns out to be her uncle Nazario's?"

"God help her!"

"No, woman, it's not her uncle Nazario's, no way! It's those damned Federales, curse 'em all!"

The old women's racket eventually wakes Demetrio up.

They quiet down. Then Señora Pachita reaches into her bosom and brings out a *palomo*[3]— the small pigeon's beak is open and it is barely breathing—and says:

"Oh, tha's right, I nearly forgot, I came to bring the señor these substances. But if he's bein' looked after by a doctor . . ."

"What you brought there won't do nothin', Señora Pachita. Tha's somethin' ya rub on the skin."

"Señor, forgive how poor and how little this is, this gift I bring you," said the wrinkled old woman, drawing close to Demetrio. "There's nothin' like this substance for blood 'morrhages."

Demetrio quickly nodded his approval. They had already

put slices of alcohol-soaked bread on his stomach, and even though they cooled off his belly when they were removed, he still felt very feverish inside.

"Go ahead, Señora Remigia. Go ahead and do it, since ya know it so good," the other women said.

Señora Remigia pulled a long, curved knife typically used to slice cactus fruit out of a reed sheath. Then she grabbed the small pigeon in one hand, held it just above Demetrio's belly, and slashed it in half with a single swipe of the blade, as skillfully as a surgeon.

"In the name of Jesus, Mary, and Joseph!" Señora Remigia said, blessing the room, and very quickly applied the two halves of the pigeon, dripping warm blood, on Demetrio's abdomen.

"Now ya'll see how ya'll start feelin' a lotta relief real soon."

Obeying Señora Remigia's instructions, Demetrio remained still, his head tucked in as he lay on his side.

Then Señora Fortunata told of her troubles. She felt much goodwill toward the señores of the revolution. Three months ago the Federales had stolen her only daughter away, leaving her inconsolable and beside herself.

When Señora Fortunata began telling her story, Quail and Anastasio Montañés, sitting on their haunches at the foot of the stretcher, raised their heads and listened, their mouths hanging open. But Señora Fortunata went on to recount the story in so many details that halfway through Quail grew bored and went outside to stretch his legs in the sun. When she finally finished up—by saying in a solemn tone, "I pray to God and the Blessed Virgin Mary that you do not leave a single one of those damned Federales alive"—Demetrio, facing the wall, feeling much relief from the substances on his stomach, was thinking of the best route to proceed to Durango, while Anastasio Montañés snored as loud as a trombone.

X

"Why don't you call the *curro* and have 'im cure you, compadre Demetrio," Anastasio Montañés said to his leader, who continued to suffer strong chills and fevers every day. "If you could only see, he cured himself and he's already so much better that he's walkin' 'round without even limpin' no more."

But Venancio, who was standing by with his tins of lard and his filthy strips of rags at the ready, protested:

"I cannot be held responsible for whatever happens if anyone else lays a hand on him."

"Listen, compadre, where do you come off thinkin' you're such a great doctor? You gonna tell us you've forgotten how you came to be here with us?" Quail asked.

"Yeah, well, what I remember, Quail, is that you're with us 'cause you stole a watch and some diamond rings," Venancio responded, all worked up.

Quail burst out laughing.

"Well, at least I did that! What's worse is that you ran away from your town 'cause you poisoned your girlfriend."

"That's a lie!"

"No, you did. You gave her some Spanish flies,[1] but they didn't work . . ."

Venancio's shouts of protest were drowned out by the clamorous laughter of the other men.

A pale, grimacing Demetrio made them quiet down. He made some moaning sounds, then said:

"Well, okay then. Go on and bring me the student."

Luis Cervantes came. He uncovered Demetrio's leg, slowly and carefully examined the wound, and shook his head. The ligature, torn from a blanket, had dug into the flesh in the form of a furrow, and the bloated leg seemed about to burst. With each movement, Demetrio bit back a cry. Luis Cervantes cut the ligature, thoroughly washed out the wound, covered the thigh with long, moist linens, and cleanly bandaged everything up.

Demetrio was able to sleep through that entire afternoon and night. The next day he woke up in much better spirits.

"He has quite a light touch, that *curro*," he remarked.

Soon afterward, Venancio said,

"He's okay. But we have to remember that *curros* are like humidity, they seep through everywhere. The fruits of many a revolution have been lost because *curros* were around."

And since Demetrio blindly believed in the science of the barber, when Cervantes came to apply his treatment the next day, he said to him:

"Listen, do a good job here so that when I'm good and cured you can go on back home or wherever you want to go."

The discreet Luis Cervantes did not say anything at all.

A week passed, then another. The Federales showed no sign of life. Meanwhile, there was an abundant amount of frijoles and corn in the ranchos in the area, and the people's hatred of the Federales was such that they were more than willing to provide the rebels with shelter. So Demetrio's men waited, quite patiently, for their leader to make a complete recovery.

Luis Cervantes remained dejected and silent for many days.

But Demetrio started to grow fond of him. Then, after the treatment one day, he said to him, in jest: "From the way you're goin' about, I'm starting to think that you're in love, *curro*!"

And eventually Demetrio Macías began taking an interest in the welfare of Luis Cervantes. He asked him if the soldiers were giving him his proper rations of meat and milk. So Cervantes had to tell him that he was eating only what the gentle old women of the rancho were giving him, and that everyone was still looking at him as an unknown or an intruder.

"They're good muchachos, *curro*," Demetrio replied. "The key is to know their way. Startin' tomorrow you'll have everything you need. You'll see."

Sure enough, things started to change that very day. Later

that evening some of Macías's men were lying on the stony ground, looking up at the clouds of twilight as if they were gigantic blood clots, listening to the stories Venancio recounted from some of the most charming episodes in *The Wandering Jew*. Many, lulled by the barber's sweet voice, dozed off and began to snore. But Luis Cervantes, after listening attentively to the story, which ended with some strange anticlerical comments, said emphatically:

"Tha's admirable. You have quite a beautiful talent."

"It's not that bad," Venancio replied, himself quite convinced of it. "But my parents died, so I was unable to go on and continue my studies."

"That does not matter in the least. Once our cause is victorious, you will be able to obtain your degree very easily. Two or three weeks of serving as an attendant at a hospital, a good recommendation from our leader Macías . . . and you shall be a doctor. You have such skill that it will all come as easy as a game to you!"

From that night on, Venancio differentiated himself from the others by no longer calling him *curro*. Instead, it was Luisito this and Luisito that.

XI

"Listen, *curro*, I was wantin' to tell ya a little somethin'," Camila said one morning when Luis Cervantes entered the hut to get some boiled water to cleanse his foot.

The girl had been restless for several days. All the attention she had been lavishing on him and her countless insinuations had finally started to annoy the young man. He suddenly interrupted his task, stood up, looked straight into her eyes, and replied:

"Well, okay. What did you want to say to me?"

At that point Camila felt her tongue turn into a wet rag and was unable to say anything. Her face lit up as red as madroño[1] berries; she shrugged her shoulders, and bent her head forward until her chin rested on her bare chest. Then, without moving, she cast her gaze, as steady as an idiot's, at the wound on the young man's leg, and said in a very weak voice:

"Look at how purty it's a-healin' already. It looks as purty as a Spanish rose."

Luis Cervantes knit his brows with evident anger and turned his attention again to his treatment, and ceased paying her any more heed.

When he finished, Camila had disappeared.

The girl was nowhere to be seen for three days after that. Señora Agapita, her mother, was the one who received Luis Cervantes when he came to their hut, and she was the one who boiled the water and the strips of linen for him. He was very careful not to ask anything about the girl. But three days later Camila was back again, with even more beating around the bush and lavishing attention upon him than before.

Distracted, Luis Cervantes treated Camila indifferently, which only served to further embolden the girl. She finally spoke up again:

"Listen, *curro*. I was wantin' to tell ya a little somethin'. Listen, *curro*. Just one thing. I'd like you teach me the words to 'La Adelita.'[2] So that . . . Can ya guess what for? So I can sing it and sing it when ya all leave, when ya're no longer 'round, when ya're already so far away, so far . . . that ya won't even remember me no more."

The effect of her words on Luis Cervantes was like that of a steel point scratching against glass.

But not noticing, she continued as ingenuously as before.

"Well, *curro*, if ya only knew. If ya was to see how mean that ol' man leader of yours is. First of all there's what happened to me with 'im. Ya know that this Demetrio doesn't want no one but my mamma to make 'im his food and no one to take it to 'im but me. Well, okay, so the other day I go in with his atole,[3] and guess what that ol' devil goes and does? Yup, sure 'nough, he reaches out and grabs my hand and squeezes it hard, real hard. Then he starts to pinch my legs and my behind. Ah, but ya shoulda seen what I did then! I says then: 'Whoa there, ya're worse than bad! Lay still, stop that! Ya're worse than bad, ya wicked devil! Let go of me, let go of me, ya shameless ol' man!' And I back away and get out of his grasp and I'm off and runnin' outside at full speed. What d'ya make of that, *curro*?"

Camila had never seen Luis Cervantes laugh so heartily.

"But is it true, is everything you are telling me true?" he asked her.

Camila was thoroughly disconcerted and unable to respond. Cervantes continued to laugh loudly, and repeated his question. She felt even more uneasy and worried, and her voice cracked as she replied:

"Yes, it's true. And tha's what I been tryin' to tell ya. Doesn't that make ya angry and wanna do somethin' about it, *curro*?"

Camila glanced up at Luis Cervantes, staring once again with adoration at his ruddy, radiant face, at his soft and expressive light green eyes, at his pinkish cheeks smooth as a porcelain doll's, at the softness of his slightly curled blond hair, and at the glow of his delicate white skin showing above his collar and outside the sleeves of his coarse wool shirt.

"So what in the world are you waiting for then, dummy? If the leader wants you, what else are you waiting for?"

Camila felt a welling up in her chest, rising to her throat, nearly choking her. She pressed her fists hard against her squinting eyes to stop the tears starting to flow from them. Then she wiped the moisture away from her cheeks with the back of her hand and ran away as quickly as a musk deer, just as she had done three days ago.

XII

Demetrio's wound was healed. They were starting to discuss their plans for heading north, where it was said that the revolutionaries had triumphed against the Federales everywhere along the line. Then an event occurred that sped things along. One cool afternoon Luis Cervantes was sitting on a peak overlooking the Sierra, gazing out into the distance, daydreaming, bored, killing time. At the foot of the narrow summit, Pancracio and Lard were playing cards, sitting like lizards between a thicket of rockroses and the banks of the river. Anastasio Montañés was watching the game without much interest, when all of a sudden he turned his black-bearded face and his sweet eyes toward Luis Cervantes, and said:

"Why are you so sad, *curro*? What're you thinkin' so much about? Come over 'ere, move closer, let's talk."

Luis Cervantes did not move. But Anastasio went over and sat next to him in a friendly manner.

"You miss all the sound and excitement of your city, don't ya? I can tell you're one of those fancy shoes and bow-tie kinda men. Look, *curro*, see the way I am here, all dirty and wearin' these torn rags for clothes? Well, I'm not what I seem to be. You don't believe me? Well, I don't have no needs. I own ten yokes of oxen back home. Really, I do! You can go ask my compadre Demetrio. I harvested my ten acres last year. You don't believe me? Look, *curro*, I really like fighting the Federales, and tha's why they hate me so much. Last time, eight months ago already (which is the same amount of time that I've been wanderin' 'round here), I stabbed me a little fascist captain (God help me), right here, smack in the middle of his gut. But, really, I don't have no needs. I'm out 'ere 'cause of that. And so I can give a hand to my compadre Demetrio."

"Oh, sweet beauty of my life!" Lard shouted out excitedly after drawing a card, and put down a twenty-cent silver coin on the ace of spades.

"So ya think I'm not much for gamblin', *curro*! Wanna bet somethin'? Come on. Check this out. This leather snake has a little rattle left to it!" Anastasio said, shaking his belt and making the silver coins in it ring out.

Pancracio flipped over the next card, another ace came up, and a dispute broke out. Accusations, shouts, then insults. Pancracio turned his stony face toward Lard, who glared back with his serpent eyes and began to shake as if he were having an epileptic fit. They were one move away from coming to blows. Their own verbal barbs being insufficiently sharp, they added the naming of their fathers and mothers to the mix in the richest embroidering of indecencies.

But nothing came of it. After the insults ran their course, the game was called off; they placed an arm around each other's shoulders peacefully and walked off together to drink some aguardiente.[1]

"I don't like gettin' into these fights with my tongue, either. It's ugly, isn't it, *curro*? Really, no one has ever gone and insulted my family. I like to make sure that I'm respected. That's why you'll never see me goin' 'round mockin' no one. Listen, *curro*," Anastasio said, suddenly interrupting himself. He stood up, put his hand above his eyes, and added: "What's that cloud of dust rising over there, behind that small hill? Hell! Here come the conservative mongrels! And here we are, completely unprepared! Come on, *curro*, let's go tell the muchachos."

Their news was met with great cheer.

"Let's go get 'em!" Pancracio was the first to exclaim.

"Yes, let's go get 'em. What can they have that we don't!"

But the enemy turned out to be a small herd of burros and two muleteers.

"Stop 'em anyway. They're highlanders and must have some news," Demetrio said.

And was the news they brought ever amazing! The Federales had fortified El Grillo and La Bufa, the hills surrounding Zacatecas.[2] It was said that this was Huerta's last stand, and everyone predicted that the plaza would soon fall. All the families were running away as quickly as they could, heading south. The trains were overflowing with people. And since there were not enough carriages and carts on the main roads, many had panicked and were fleeing on foot, even lugging their possessions on their backs. The revolutionary leader Pánfilo Natera[3] was said to be gathering his people in Fresnillo, near the city of Zacatecas, and everyone was saying that the Federales were already "wearing pants that were getting too big for them."

"The fall of Zacatecas will be Huerta's *Requiescat in pace*," Luis Cervantes assured with extraordinary ardor. "We must get there and join the ranks of General Natera before the attack."

Noticing the wonderment that his words produced on the faces of Demetrio and his comrades, Cervantes realized that he was still a mister nobody with the group.

The next day, however, when the men headed out to look for good mounts for their march, Demetrio called Luis Cervantes and said to him:

"So you really wanna come with us, *curro*? You're water of a different river than we are, and honestly, I can't understand how ya can like this life. D'ya think that we're wanderin' around out here 'cause we like it? It's true, we enjoy all the noise and excitement, why deny it, but it's not just that. Sit down, *curro,* sit down, let me tell ya all about it. D'ya know why I rose up in rebellion? Listen up, I'll tell ya. Before the revolution, I even had my own little corner of land to sow, and if it hadn't been for the run-in that I had with Don Mónico, the cacique of Moyahua, d'ya know what I'd be doin' right now? I'd be rushin' about, preparin' my team of oxen to sow my land. Pancracio, go get us two bottles of beer, one for me and one for the *curro* here. For heaven's sakes. A little drink won't hurt me no more now, will it?"

XIII

"I'm from Limón, a place very close to Moyahua, right in the middle of the Juchipila canyon. I had my house, my cows, and a small piece of land to sow. In other words, I had everythin' I needed. Well, señor, us rancheros we have this custom where we go into town once a week. Ya hear mass, ya listen to the sermon, then ya go to the plaza, buy your onions, your tomatoes, and everything else ya might need. Then you go to Primitivo López's tavern to take a break from things. Ya have a *the catalyst / back story*

little drink, sometimes more than one, sometimes ya have a bit too much, and then the drink goes to your head, and ya have ya a good ol' time, and ya laugh, and ya shout and sing even, if ya bloody well feel like it. Everything's good and no one's doin' no one any harm.

"But then they start to bother ya, the policeman keeps comin' by, walkin' to and fro, peekin' in through the door, and the chief of police or the deputies decide to ruin your day. Needless to say, compadre, ya don't have ice water in your veins, ya're made outta flesh and bones, and ya have a soul, after all, ya start to get angry, ya stand up for yourself and say your piece! If they get what ya're sayin', all's well and good, they let ya be, and that's the end of it. But sometimes they go and talk all tough and start hittin', and ya're pretty hotheaded as it is, and ya don't appreciate it none when someone tries to show ya up. And, yes señor, before ya know it, the knife comes out, or ya draw your gun. And then ya're off and running all through the Sierra till they forget all about that poor li'l corpse of theirs!

"Well, what happened with Don Mónico then, ya ask? He was a damn ol' fool, but not so foolish with me. What happened to him is much less than what happened to many others, I can tell ya that. I spit on his beard 'cause he wouldn't mind his own business, and tha's that, there's nothin' else to tell. After that he had just about all the federation come down on me. Ya must know the story of what happened in Mexico City, the one about how they killed Señor Madero and some other man, Félix or Felipe Díaz or somethin' like that?[1] Well, this Don Mónico goes personally to Zacatecas to bring back a whole army squadron to arrest me. Sayin' that I was a Maderista[2] and that I was about to rise up and join the revolution.[3] But since I have plenty of friends, someone came to tell me in time, and when the Federales came to Limón, I had already run off. Then my compadre Anastasio joined me, since he had killed someone, an' then Pancracio, Quail, and many more friends an' other men I didn't even know at that point. After that more an' more men have

What happened to Macías' wife?

joined us, an' now here we are, as you see us. We go along fightin' as best as we can."

"Dear leader," Luis Cervantes said after a few minutes of silence and reflection. "As you already know, Natera's men are gathered near here, in Juchipila. It behooves us to go and join them before they take Zacatecas. We should present ourselves before the general and—"

"I have no talent for that kind of thing. I don't like to bow down to no one."

"But if you stay out here alone, with just a handful of men, you will never be more than a small-time rebel leader. The revolution will triumph, that is for certain. And once it is over, they will say to you the same thing that they said to those who helped Madero.[4] They will say: 'Friends, thank you very much. Now ya can go back home—'"

"But I don't want nothin' other than that. I just want 'em to leave me in peace so I can go back home."

"Yes, yes, I'm getting to that. I haven't finished yet. For his part, Madero said, 'You have helped carry me to the presidency of the republic. You have risked your lives, with the imminent danger of leaving widows and orphans behind in misery. And now that I have achieved my goal, go on back to your picks and shovels, go on back to your daily struggles, always hungry and half-naked, as you were before. Meanwhile, those of us up here will go ahead and make a few million pesos for ourselves.'"

Demetrio shook his head, smiled, and scratched himself.

"Luisito has spoken the God's honest truth!" the barber Venancio exclaimed enthusiastically.

"As I was saying," Luis Cervantes continued. "Once the revolution comes to an end, everything will come to an end. And what a pity it will be for all those lives cut short, for all those widows and orphans, for all that spilled blood! All of that and for what? So that a handful of indolent rogues can grow rich, while everything else remains the same as before, or even worse? Since you are unselfish, you say: 'I have no ambition other than to return to my land.' But is it just to deprive your wife and children of the fortune that divine providence now lays in your hands? Would it be just to abandon your country now, at these solemn times, precisely when the motherland will need all the selflessness of its most humble children to save her, so she will not fall again into the hands of the caciques, those eternal thieves and murderers? We must not forget the most sacred things a man has in this world: his family and his country!"

Macías smiled. His eyes sparkled.

"So . . . So ya think it would be good to go and join Natera, *curro*?"

"Not only good," Venancio exclaimed, trying to sound persuasive. "But indispensable, Demetrio."

"Esteemed leader," Cervantes continued, "ever since we met, you and I have gotten along very well, and I have grown to care for you more and more as I have come to know how valuable you are to the revolution. Allow me now to be entirely frank. I believe that you do not yet understand your true, your high, your most noble mission. You are a modest man, without any ambition. You have not yet opened your eyes and seen the very important role that you are to play in this revolution. You are not really out here just because of the cacique don Mónico. You have risen up against the cacique system itself, the system that is devastating the entire nation. We are constitutive pieces of a great social movement that will lead to the exaltation of our motherland. We are instruments of destiny for the revindication of the sacred rights of the people. We are not fighting in order to defeat one miserable murderer. We are fighting a fight against tyranny itself. And that is what it means to fight for one's principles, to have ideals. That is what Villa, Natera, and Carranza are fighting for.[5] And that is what we are fighting for."

"Yes, yes. Exactly what I was thinking," Venancio said, nearly beside himself.

"Pancracio, go on, bring us two more beers."

XIV

"If ya could see how good the *curro* explains things, compadre Anastasio," Demetrio said, reflecting on what he had been able to discern from Luis Cervantes's words that morning.

"Yes, I heard 'im," Anastasio replied. "Truth is, he's one of those who understands things good, since he knows how to read and write. But the thing that I don't really get, compadre, is how we're supposed to go and present ourselves to Señor Natera since there's so few of us."

"H'm, that's the least of it! From now on we're gonna do things a little different. I heard tell how Crispín Robles goes into every town he finds, takes all the weapons and horses they have there, lets all the prisoners outta the jail, and just like that he has more than enough men with 'im. You'll see. Truth is, compadre Anastasio, that we've wasted a lot of time already. Seems hard to believe that we needed this *curro* to show up and lecture us just to get us to wake up and see what's what."

"Tha's what happens when ya know how to read and write!"

The two sighed sadly.

Luis Cervantes and the other men entered to ask when they would be leaving.

"Tomorrow. We're headin' out in the mornin'," Demetrio said without any hesitation.

Quail then proposed that they bring in music from the neighboring town so they could have a farewell dance. His idea was welcomed with much fervor and excitement.

"Well, we may be leavin'," Pancracio exclaimed, and let out a howl. "But at least I'm not leavin' alone this time. I have my love and I'm bringin' 'er with me."

Demetrio said that he too would very much like to take with him a young lady upon whom he had laid his eyes. But he added that he really did not want his men to leave behind any dark memories, as the Federales always did.

genuinely good person. considerate

"You won't have to wait long. Everything will be arranged when we come back," Luis Cervantes whispered to him.

"How's that?" Demetrio asked. "Didn't I hear that you and Camila . . ."

"There is no truth in that, dear leader. She loves you, but she is afraid of you."

"Really, *curro*?"

"Yes. But I think what you say is very much the case. We must not leave the wrong impression behind. When we return in triumph, everything will be different. Everyone will even be thanking you for this gesture then."

"Oh, *curro*. You sure are a sharp one!" Demetrio replied, smiling and patting Luis Cervantes on the back.

As nightfall neared, Camila walked down to the river to get water, as usual. Luis Cervantes was walking up the same path from the opposite direction.

Camila felt her heart racing in her chest.

But Luis Cervantes suddenly disappeared around a bend in the path, behind a large boulder, perhaps without even noticing that she was approaching.

As on every other day at that time of the late afternoon, twilight spread its dusky hue over the calcined stones, the sunburned branches, and the dried-out moss. A warm, rustling wind blew softly and swayed the lanceolate leaves in the cornfield. Everything was the same as always. But Camila sensed something different, something strange in the stones, the dry branches, the fragrant air, and the fallen leaves: as if all those things were now suffused with an unusual sadness.

She walked around a gigantic eroded boulder and ran suddenly into Luis Cervantes perched atop a large stone, where he was sitting with his hat off and his legs dangling down.

"Hey, *curro*. At least come on over an' say good-bye to me."

Obligingly enough, Luis Cervantes got off the rock and joined her.

"Ya're so arrogant! Was I so bad to ya that ya don't even talk to me?"

"Why do you say that to me, Camila? You have been very good to me. Better than a friend, in fact. You have taken care of me like a sister. I leave you very grateful and will always remember what you have done for me."

"Ya liar!" Camila said, now full of joy. "And if I hadn't said anything to ya just now?"

"I was planning on saying thank you this evening at the dance."

"What dance? If there's a dance, I'm not goin'."

"Why are you not going?"

"'Cause I can't stand to look at that mean ol' man . . . at that Demetrio."

"How silly! Listen, he really loves you, Camila. Do not miss this opportunity, for it shall not come by in your lifetime again. Do not be a fool, Demetrio will be a general before long, he will be very, very rich. He will have many horses, many jewels, very fancy dresses, elegant houses, and plenty of money to spend on anything he wants. Imagine what it would be like to be by his side!"

Camila looked up at the blue sky, trying to hide her eyes from him. Up above, a dry leaf broke from a treetop and drifted slowly down, falling at her feet like a small, dead butterfly. She bent over and grabbed it gently. Then, without looking toward him, she murmured:

"Oh, *curro*. If ya only knew how bad it feels when ya say all those things to me. Ya're the one that I love, don't ya know. You and only you. Go away, *curro*. Go away, I don't know why I get so embarrassed like this. Go away, go away!"

And she quickly crumbled up the leaf in her trembling hand and tossed it away, and then covered her face with her apron.

When she looked up again, Luis Cervantes was nowhere to be seen.

Camila got up and started walking down the path toward the creek again. Now it looked as if the water was sprinkled with fine particles of carmine, as if a sky of colors and sharp peaks of light and valleys of shadows stirred about in its waters. Myriads of luminous insects blinked above a pool near the water's edge. And at the bottom, the reflection just above the smooth, round pebbles reproduced Camila's yellow blouse with its green ribbons, her white skirt, her clean and finely combed hair, and her smooth eyebrows and forehead—exactly as she had prepared herself to please Luis Cervantes.

And she burst into tears again.

In the thicket of rockroses the frogs sang the implacable melancholy of the hour.

Swaying back and forth on a dry branch, a dove cried as well.

(el paloma (healing))

XV

There was much merrymaking and a lot of very good mezcal[1] at the dance.

"I wish Camila was here," Demetrio said loudly.

Everyone looked around for Camila.

"She's sick, she has a real bad headache," Señora Agapita said in a harsh voice, irritated by the mean looks she was getting from everyone.

Later, as the fandango was coming to an end, Demetrio, swaying a bit as he spoke, thanked the good neighbors who had given them such generous shelter, and promised that he would keep them all in mind once the revolution triumphed. He concluded with: "Bed and prison, that's where ya always know who your real friends are."

"May God hold you in his blessed hand," an old woman said.

"May God bless you and lead you down the righteous path," a few others said.

And a very drunk María Antonia added:

"May ya come back soon. But real, real soon now!"

The next day, María Antonia who, despite being pockmarked and having a lazy eye, had a very bad reputation—so bad that everyone said there was no man who had not taken a turn with her behind the thicket of rockroses by the riverbanks—yelled at Camila:

"Hey, you! What's this cryin' all about? What're ya doin' in the corner with that shawl wrapped 'round your head? Hey? Don't tell me that ya're cryin' now? Look at your eyes, girl. Ya look like a witch already. Go on. There's nothin' to get all upset about. Ya know there's no pain that ever lasts no more than three days."

Señora Agapita knit her brows and mumbled something incomprehensible under her breath.

The women were actually quite upset by the departure of Demetrio and his men. Even the men, despite the insults they muttered between their teeth, lamented that they would no longer be eating lamb and sheep for dinner. That had been the life indeed: eating and drinking to their hearts' delight, and sleeping long siestas in the shade of the large boulders with their legs stretched out while the clouds drifted slowly across the sky overhead.

"Look at 'em again. There they go," María Antonia shouted. "They look like toy soldiers arranged on a cupboard."

In the distance, Macías's men could be seen atop the edge of a summit—out where the rugged ground and the chaparral began to merge into a bluish, velvety horizon—cut out against the sky's sapphire radiance. A warm breeze carried the faint, intermittent melody of "La Adelita" back to the huts.

Camila had come out when she had heard María Antonia's voice. Seeing them one last time, she was unable to control herself, and once again broke out in sobs.

María Antonia laughed loudly and walked away.

"Someone has cast the evil eye on my daughter," murmured Señora Agapita, perplexed.

She thought quietly for a while. Then, after going over it carefully in her mind, she made a decision. She reached up to a spike nailed into a post in her hut, between the image of Christ and one of the Virgin of Jalpa, and grabbed the raw leather strap that her husband used to yoke the oxen. And folding the long strap in half, she gave Camila a thorough thrashing to drive away the evil spirits. *WTF*

As he rode on his chestnut horse, Demetrio felt rejuvenated. His eyes had recovered their peculiar metallic sparkle, and the red, hot blood was flowing again through his coppery, pure-race indigenous cheeks.

The men all filled their lungs deeply, as if they were trying to breathe in the vast horizon, the immensity of the sky, the blueness of the mountains, and the fresh air infused with the sweet fragrances of the Sierra. They galloped on their horses as if they could thus take possession of all the land with their unrestrained running. Who among them thought then of the severe chief of police, of the grumbling gendarme, or of the pompous cacique? Who then thought any more of their wretched shack of a house, where one lives like a slave, always under the watch of the owner or of the surly, cruel majordomo? Who among them thought at that point of always having to be up before sunrise, with shovel and basket in hand, or lugging plow and goad, ready to go out and earn one's daily serving of atole and frijoles?

They sang, they laughed, and they hooted, drunk with the sun, the air, and life itself.

The Indian pranced forward on his horse; flashing his white teeth, he told jokes and acted like a clown.

"Listen, Pancracio," he asked very seriously. "In a letter I got here my wife has notified me that we have another child now. How can that be? I haven't seen her since the days of Señor Madero!"

"Nah, tha's nothin'. When ya left 'er the bun was already in the oven!"

Everyone bursts out in loud laughter. Everyone except the Indian, who starts singing in a falsetto voice, grave and aloof and horribly off-key:

> *I gave her a penny*
> *but she said no, no, no . . .*

I gave her a nickel
but she wanted more.
She begged and she begged
until I gave her a dime.
Oh, ungrateful women
showin' no consideration at all!

The clamoring finally ceased when the sun began to beat down on them.

All day long they rode along the canyon. All day long they climbed up and down sloping hills, dirty, cropped hills like scabbed heads, hills always endlessly followed by more hills.

In the late afternoon, they made out the vague outline of several tall church towers against the blue-ridged mountains in the distance, and beyond this, a road with swirling white dust and gray telegraph poles.

They headed toward the main road, where they saw the shape of a man sitting on his haunches off to one side. They approached him. He was a ragged, ugly-looking old man working hard as he tried to repair a leather sandal with a dull knife. Near him grazed a donkey loaded with a bale of hay.

Demetrio asked: "What're ya doin' here, gramps?"

"I'm headin' to town, bringin' alfalfa for my cow."

"How many Federales in town?"

"Yup . . . there's a few, I think no more than a dozen."

The old man started talking. He spoke of very grave rumors. That Obregón was already laying siege to Guadalajara; that Carrera Torres had taken San Luis Potosí; and that Pánfilo Natera was in Fresnillo.[2]

"Well then," Demetrio said. "You can go on 'head and head back into town. But ya better be careful and not tell no one who ya just saw out here, 'cause if ya do I'll blow your brains out myself. I'll find you even if ya go and hide in the center of the earth."

"What d'ya say, muchachos?" Demetrio inquired after the old man had left.

"Let's go get 'em! Let's go kill every single one of those conservative mongrels!" Demetrio's men exclaimed.

They counted the cartridges and the hand grenades that Owl[3] had built with fragments of iron pipes and brass knobs.

"It's not much," Anastasio observed. "But we'll trade 'em in for real rifles soon 'nough."

They pressed forward anxiously, spurring the thin flanks of their fatigued nags.

But Demetrio's imperious voice stopped them. Following their leader's orders, they made camp at the foothill of a rise, protected by a thick growth of huisache trees. Without unsaddling their horses, every man sought a rock to lay his head.

XVI

Demetrio Macías gave the marching orders at midnight.

The town was one or two leagues away. They were going to strike the Federales at dawn. The sky was clouded over and only a handful of stars shone above, but occasionally there was a reddish flash of lightning that lit up the entire night.

Luis Cervantes asked Demetrio if it might not behoove them—so as to be even more successful in their attack—to find a guide, or at the very least to gather the town's topographic details and the precise situation of the barracks of the Federales.

"No, *curro*," Demetrio replied, smiling with a disdainful expression. "We hit 'em when they least expect it, and tha's that. Tha's how we've always done it, many times before, and it's how we'll always do it. Ever seen how squirrels stick their heads outta their holes if ya fill 'em up with water? Well, these damned little conservative mongrels will come out just as stunned when they hear the first shots. They'll come out, and we'll be there ready to use their heads as target practice."

"And what if the old man who gave us that information yesterday was lying? What if they turn out to have fifty men instead of twenty? What if that old man was a spy put out there by the Federales?"

"This *curro* here is startin' to get all scared already!" Anastasio Montañés said.

"Yes, handling a rifle is not like boilin' water and puttin' on bandages and givin' enemas, is it now, *curro*?" Pancracio asked.

"H'm, come on!" the Indian said. "Too much talk already. All this over a dozen scared rats!"

"Soon enough we'll find out whether our mothers gave birth to real men or what," Lard added.

When they reached the edge of the small town, Venancio went on ahead and knocked on the door of the first small house he found.

"Where's the barracks?" he demanded of the man who stepped outside, barefoot, wearing a torn poncho around his otherwise bare chest.

"The barracks is just down there by the plaza, sir," he answered.

But as none of them knew where "down there by the plaza" was, Venancio forced the man to walk out in front of their column and show them the way.

Trembling with fear, the unfortunate wretch exclaimed that what they were making him do was outrageous.

"I'm just a poor peasant, señor. I have a wife and small children."

"And what are mine, dogs?" Demetrio replied.

Then he ordered:

"Very quiet now, on the ground, single file, down the middle of the street."

The broad quadrangular church dome rose up above the other houses of the town.

"See there, señores? The plaza is in front of the church. Ya just walk a little farther down from there and ya'll run straight into the barracks."

The man then knelt down and begged them to let him go back home. But without answering, Pancracio struck the man in the chest with the butt of his rifle and made him continue.

"How many soldiers are stationed here?" Luis Cervantes asked the man.

"Sir, I don't wanna lie to ya, your grace. But truth is, truth is there's a whole lot of 'em there."

Luis Cervantes looked at Demetrio, but Macías pretended not to have heard anything.

They soon reached a small plaza, where they were met by a deafening discharge of rifles. Startled, Demetrio's chestnut-colored horse reared, staggered on its hind legs, folded its forelegs, and fell down kicking. Owl let out a shrill cry and rolled off his horse, which bolted madly toward the middle of the plaza.

A new round of rifle shots was fired toward them, and the man who had guided them spread his arms out and fell backward without exhaling a sound.

Anastasio Montañés quickly lifted Demetrio up and carried him over his shoulder. The others had already retreated and were hiding behind the walls of the surrounding houses.

"Señores, señores," a common townsman said, sticking his head out from a large doorway. "You should circle 'round and get 'em from behind the chapel. They're all in there. Go back down this same street, turn left at the first corner, then ya'll reach a small alley, and then ya'll go through that till ya reach the back of the chapel."

At that point an incessant round of pistol fire began raining down on them. It came from the nearby terraces.

"Oh," the man said, "those aren't bitin' spiders fallin' down on us. That's the *curros*. Come inside here till they leave. They'll run away soon, those *curros*, they're afraid of their own shadows."

"How many conservative mongrels are in town?" Demetrio asked.

"There were no more than a dozen or so here before. But last night they were real afraid of somethin' and they used the telegraph to call for reinforcements. So who knows how many are in town now! But it doesn't matter if there's a lot of 'em. Most of 'em were enlisted by the draft, and it doesn't take much of nothin' for 'em to turn and run and leave their leaders behind. My brother was caught by the damned draft and they have 'im in there with 'em. I'll go with ya, I'll give ya a sign, and ya'll see how all the men that was drafted come over to this side as soon as ya attack. And then we can get rid of the officers once and for all. If ya could just give me some kind of weapon, señor, I'd join ya at once."

"We don't have no rifles left, brother. But this oughtta be good for somethin'," Anastasio Montañés said, handing the man a couple of hand grenades.

The leader of the Federales was a very presumptuous young blond man with waxed mustaches. At first, when he did not know the exact number of men who had assaulted them, he had remained extremely quiet and cautious. But now that the enemy had been so successfully turned back, and they had not even given them a chance to fire a single shot, he started making unwise shows of courage and taking extraordinary risks. While all the other soldiers barely dared to stick their heads out from behind the stone pillars to look toward the enemy, the leader of the Federales went out in the bright early morning and exhibited his elegant, slender figure, his long cape occasionally waving behind him in the breeze.

"Ah, this reminds me of our glorious military uprising!"

Since his military career was limited to just one adventure—the time he had participated as a cadet at the School of Officers when the revolt against President Madero had broken out—every time the slightest reason arose, he would invariably recall the deeds at the Ciudadela.[1]

"Lieutenant Campos," he ordered emphatically. "Take ten men and finish off those bandits hiding down there. Go and get those dirty, rotten dogs down below! They only act brave when it comes time to shooting cows and stealing chickens!"

A peasant appeared under the arch of a small door. He came with the news that the assailants had retreated to a corral, where it would be very easy to seize all of them at once.

This message came from the distinguished citizens of the town, who had taken their stations on their own terraces, determined not to let the enemy escape.

"I myself will go finish them off," the officer said vehemently. But almost immediately he changed his mind. Backing away from the door, he said:

"They may be expecting reinforcements, and it would be imprudent for me to abandon my post. Lieutenant Campos, you go and bring them back to me alive, so we can have them shot by firing squad later this very day at noon, when everyone in town is coming out of high mass. I shall make fine examples of these bandits! But if you cannot capture them alive, Lieutenant Campos, then finish them all off. No one is to get out of this town alive. Understood?"

And being well satisfied with himself, he began to pace back and forth and to think about the official dispatch he would write in his rendering of the events. "To His Honor the Minister of War, Most Esteemed General Don Aureliano Blanquet.[2] Mexico City. It is my pleasure, General, to bring to Your Excellency's attention that at sunrise on the . . . day of this month, a party of five hundred men under the leadership of H . . . sought to attack this plaza. With the force necessitated by the occasion, I gathered our troops at the elevated areas of the town. The attack commenced at dawn and lasted for a duration of more than two hours of sustained gunfire. Despite the enemy's numerical superiority, under my leadership, we managed to punish them severely and defeat them unequivocally. Their dead numbered at twenty, and even more were injured, judging by the trail of blood they left behind in their precipitous retreat. Among our ranks we had the good fortune of not being hit by a single bullet. It is my pleasure to congratulate you, esteemed Minister, for this triumph on behalf of the troops of the Republic. Long live His Honor General Don Victoriano Huerta![3] Long live Mexico!

"After which," he went on in his mind, "my promotion to major will be assured." And he clenched his fists with joy just as a report of gunfire went off, leaving his ears ringing.

XVII

"So ya're sayin' that if we can get through this corral we'd come straight out into the alley?" Demetrio asked.

"Yes. Except that after the corral there's a house, then another corral, and then a store after that," the townsman replied.

Demetrio scratched his head thoughtfully. But his decision came at once.

"Can ya get a pick, or a pickax, or somethin' like that, to break a hole through that wall there?"

"Yes, they have all of that here. But—"

"But what? Where do they keep everythin'?"

"Sure the equipment's all here, I tell ya. But all these houses here belong to the owner, my boss . . ."

Without listening any further, Demetrio walked to the room indicated as the place where the tools were kept.

From there, the entire operation took but a few minutes.

Once they were out in the alleyway, they ran in single file, staying close to the walls for cover, until they reached the area behind the church.

They had to jump over a short adobe fence before they could scale the rear wall of the chapel.

"Heaven help us," Demetrio thought. He was the first to climb over.

The others followed at once, climbing like monkeys until they reached the top, their hands streaked with dirt and blood. After that it was much easier: deep, worn steps along the stonework allowed them to quickly mount the chapel wall, and then the church vault itself hid them from the soldiers below.

"Hold on there for a minute," the townsman said. "Let me go and see about my brother. I'll give ya a sign, and then . . . ya'all pounce on the officers. Okay?"

But by then no one was paying any more attention to him.

For a moment Demetrio looked at his men crowded in the church tower around him, behind the iron rail. Then he contemplated the black wavering of the soldiers' dark coats below.

Smiling and satisfied, he exclaimed to his men:

"Now!"

Twenty grenades exploded simultaneously in the middle of the Federales. Overcome with fear, they jumped to attention, their eyes wide open. But before they had a chance to recover from their surprise, another twenty grenades exploded, creating a tremendous clamor, leaving dead and wounded men scattered about.

"No, not yet! Not yet! I can't see my brother yet . . ." the townsman pleaded in anguish.

An old sergeant scolds and insults the soldiers, hoping to reorganize the troop and save the day, but in vain. The scene is that of rats running about in a trap. Some try to storm the base of the stairs and there they fall, gunned down by Demetrio and his men. Others throw themselves at the feet of the twenty-some-odd specters—their heads and chests dark as iron, their legs clad in torn long white trousers—above them but are riddled with bullets down to their sandals. While still others, in the bell tower, struggle to get out from under the dead who have fallen upon them.

"Dear leader!" Luis Cervantes exclaims, extremely alarmed. "We are out of grenades and the rifles are down in the corral! We are doomed!"

Demetrio smiles and unsheathes a knife with a long, shiny blade. Instantly steel gleams in the hands of his twenty soldiers, some blades long and tapering to a sharp point, others wide as the palm of a hand, many heavy as machetes.

"The spy!" Luis Cervantes cries out, triumphantly. "I told you so!"

"Don't kill me, Papi!" the old sergeant implores at Demetrio's feet, just as Macías raises his blade in the air.

The old man turns his wrinkled indigenous face toward Macías. Demetrio recognizes the man who betrayed them from the night before.

Luis Cervantes quickly averts his gaze, horrified. The steel blade hits ribs that go *crack, crack,* and the old man falls back, his arms spread wide open, his eyes full of terror.

"No, not my brother! Not him, don't kill 'im, he's my brother!" the townsman shouts, mad with fear as he sees Pancracio jump on a Federale.

It is too late. In one fell swoop Pancracio has slit the man's throat, and now two scarlet streams gush out as if from a fountain.

"Kill the soldiers! Kill the conservative mongrels!"

Pancracio and Lard distinguish themselves in the butchery, finishing off the wounded. Montañés drops his hands, completely exhausted. His face still has that sweet look in his eyes, glowing with the ingenuousness of a child and the amorality of a jackal.

"I gotta live one here," Quail shouts out.

Pancracio runs toward him. It is the short blond captain—now pale as wax—with the Frenchified mustaches. Cowering in a corner at the top of the spiral staircase, he has stopped moving, too weak to climb down or to try anything else.

Pancracio shoves him out to the edge of the platform. A blow with his knee to the captain's hips, and something like a sack of stones falls twenty meters to the atrium of the church.

"You're such an animal!" Quail exclaims. "Ya don't even know what ya just ruined. That was a fine pair of shoes I was gonna get for myself!"

The men, now bent over the dead soldiers, are taking the best clothes they can find. Then they dress themselves with the spoils, joking and laughing, thoroughly enjoying themselves.

Demetrio pushes aside the long, sweat-soaked strands of hair sticking to his forehead down to his eyes, and says:

"Now, let's go get the *curros* in town, muchachos!"

XVIII

Demetrio arrived in Fresnillo with a hundred men the same day that Pánfilo Natera was commencing his advance on the plaza of Zacatecas with his forces.[1]

The leader from Zacatecas welcomed him cordially.

"I already know of you and your men! I've already heard the news of the thrashing that you've been giving the Federales from Tepic to Durango!"[2]

Natera shook Macías's hand effusively, and Luis Cervantes declaimed:

"With men such as General Natera and Colonel Macías, our motherland will witness nothing but glory."

Demetrio immediately understood the intention behind those words as he heard himself referred to as colonel.

Wine and beer were served at once. Demetrio clinked his glass with Natera's many times. Luis Cervantes delivered a toast: "To the triumph of our cause, which is the sublime triumph of Justice. So that we may soon see realized the ideals of redemption of this, our long-suffering and noble people, and so that the same men who have watered the earth with their own blood may now be the ones who harvest the fruits that legitimately belong to them."

Natera glared sternly at the chatterbox, but only for an instant. Then, giving him his back, he began chatting with Demetrio.

One of Natera's officers had slowly approached, looking closely at Luis Cervantes. He was a young man with a sincere, cordial expression.

"Luis Cervantes?"

"Señor Solís?"

"I thought I recognized you from the moment all of you entered . . . and it is you! But even as I stand here looking at you, I do not believe it."

"Yes, it is I, believe it . . ."

"So you . . . ? Come, let us have a drink, shall we?

"Well!" Solís continued, offering Luis Cervantes a seat. "So when did you become a revolutionary, señor?"

"It has been two months now."

"Ah, that explains why you still speak with that enthusiasm and faith that we all had when we first came here!"

"Have you lost yours already, señor?"

"Listen, comrade, do not be taken aback when I address you in confidence so soon after we just meet. Around here, one misses so much speaking with people of common sense, that when such a person appears, one yearns to speak with him as anxiously as one yearns for a pitcher of cold water after walking for hours on end in the heat, under the blazing sun . . . But honestly, before we go any further, I need you to explain to me. I do not understand how the correspondent for *El País* at the time of Madero,[3] the man who wrote furious articles for *El Regional*,[4] and who so lavishly used the epithet of 'bandits' to describe us, is now fighting among our very rank and file."

"Truthfully, quite truthfully, they simply convinced me!" Cervantes replied emphatically.

"They convinced you?"

political ambiguity

Solís let out an audible sigh. He filled their glasses, and they drank.

"Have you grown tired, then, of the revolution?" Luis Cervantes asked aloofly.

"Tired? I am twenty-five years old and, as you see, I have good health to spare . . . Disillusioned? Perhaps."

"You must have your reasons . . ."

"I imagined a flowering prairie at the end of the road . . . and instead found myself in a swamp. My friend: there are events and men out here who are nothing but pure bile. And that bile drips on one's soul one drop at a time, until everything becomes soured, poisoned. Enthusiasm, dreams, ideals, joy . . . nothing! Before long none of that is left. Either one turns into a bandit just like them, or one disappears from the scene, hiding behind the walls of an impenetrable and fierce selfishness."

foreshadowing

The conversation was torture to Luis Cervantes. Hearing such words—so untimely and out of place—was physically painful to him. To avoid having to say anything, he invited Solís to recount in detail the events that had led him to such a state of disenchantment.

"Events? Insignificant ones, little things, really: facial expressions that go unnoticed by others, a brief glimmering in a pair of eyes as lips curl, the fleeting meaning of a phrase quickly left behind. Yet when these events, when these gestures and expressions logically and naturally accumulate, they constitute and integrate the grotesque, frightful grimace of a race . . . Of a race still waiting for its redemption!" Solís downed another glass of wine, paused for a long while, then continued: "You will ask me then why do I stay on with the revolution. And the answer is this: the revolution is a hurricane, and when a man surrenders himself to her, he ceases to be a man and becomes, instead, a lowly leaf blown wildly about by the winds . . ."

Demetrio Macías walked up to them, and Solís stopped talking.

"We're off, *curro* . . ."

Alberto Solís used his free-flowing words and the same deeply sincere tone to congratulate Macías effusively for his deeds in battle and for his great adventures, all of which had made him famous, known even by the men of the powerful northern division.[5]

Demetrio was charmed as he heard the recounting of his exploits, composed and embellished in such a manner that he himself almost did not recognize them. In fact, the tales sounded so good that he ended up recounting them in the same way and in the same tone, and even believing that that was how they had actually occurred.

"What a pleasant man, that General Natera!" Luis Cervantes remarked to Demetrio Macías on their way back to the tavern. "But that little Captain Solís . . . what a nuisance!"

Demetrio did not hear him. Thrilled, he grabbed one of Cervantes's arms and said softly to him:

"I'm really a colonel now, *curro*. And you, you're my secretary . . ."

Macías's men also made many new friends that night, and much mezcal and other spirits were drunk "for the pleasure of meeting you." Since not everyone is compatible and since alcohol is sometimes a bad adviser, there were naturally some disagreements as well. But everything was settled in good form and always outside the bars, the eating houses, or the brothels, so that no one was overly upset.

The following morning a few showed up dead: an old prostitute with a gunshot in her gut, and two recruits from Macías's group, their skulls riddled with bullets. Anastasio Montañés went to tell his leader, who shrugged his shoulders, and said:

"Pshaw! Have 'em buried . . ."

devalue human life, routine

XIX

"Here come the 'big hats,' they're back already," the people of Fresnillo cried when they learned that the attack of the revolutionaries on Zacatecas had failed.

They were an unruly mob of parched, filthy, barely clad men, their heads covered by palm-leaf sombreros with tall cone-shaped crowns and immense brims that hid half their faces.

Thus the mob were called big hats. And the big hats were returning as happy as when they had marched off before, plundering every town, every hacienda, every rancho, and even the most miserable hut they had found along the way.

"Who wants to buy this here machine?" one of them shouted out, beet red and exhausted from lugging the heavy weight of his "advance."[1]

It was a new typewriter; everyone was drawn to the dazzling glare reflecting off its nickel surface.

The "Oliver" had had five different owners in just one morning. It began at a value of ten pesos and depreciated by one or two pesos with each change in ownership. The truth was that it weighed too much and that no one could bear to carry it for longer than half an hour or so.

"I'll give ya a peseta for it," Quail offered.

"It's yours," the latest owner replied, quickly handing it over, clearly afraid that the other would change his mind.

For twenty-five cents, Quail had the pleasure of lifting the machine in his hands and hurling it hard against a big stone, where it shattered loudly.

This was like a signal: everyone who had been carrying heavy or awkward objects began to get rid of them, smashing them against the rocks. Shards of glass and fragments of porcelain flew about everywhere. Bulky mirrors, brass candelabra, elegant little statues, fine china, and all the other superfluous things from that day's "advance" ended up shattered and abandoned along the road.

Demetrio did not share in such joy, completely unrelated as it was to the results of the military operations. He called Montañés and Pancracio over, and said to them:

"These men don't have enough nerve. It's not that hard to take a plaza. Listen, first ya open wide like this, then ya come together, ya come together . . . and bang! And tha's it!" And he made a big, round gesture, spreading out his strong, well-defined arms; then he slowly brought them together, drawing out the motion as he spoke, until his arms were tight against his broad chest.

Anastasio and Pancracio found the explanation extremely simple and clear, and were fully convinced of what Macías was saying.

"Tha's the truth, chief! They don't have no nerve!" they said.

Demetrio's men set up camp in a corral.

When they were all lying down and yawning with fatigue, Demetrio asked, "Do ya remember Camila, compadre Anastasio?" and sighed deeply.

"Who's Camila, compadre?"

"That girl who made my food back there, in that little rancho . . ."

Anastasio shrugged as if to say: "I'm not interested in such questions about women."

"I just can't stop thinkin' about 'er," Demetrio continued, with a cigar in his mouth. "I was real bad off back then. And then I drank a jug of refreshing blue water. 'Don't ya want more?' that sweet little dark girl asked me . . . Well, that was that, I was done in by the fevers, and all it took was seein' a bowl of blue water and hearin' that soft little voice askin', 'Don't ya want more . . .' And that voice, compadre, was like a silver flute in my ears . . . Pancracio, how 'bout it, whatta'ya say? Come to that little rancho with me?"

"Listen, compadre Demetrio, I know ya don't believe me, but I have lots of experience in this question of the ladies. Ah, women! Good for a little while . . . and what a good little while! If I was to tell ya all the pocks and scratches that they've left on my scalp! The evil eye on 'em! They're the evilest of enemies. Really, compadre, don't ya believe me? That's why not even if . . . Ya know I have lots of experience with all that."

"What day should we go to the little rancho, Pancracio?" Demetrio insisted, exhaling a mouthful of gray smoke.

"All ya gotta do is say the word . . . Ya know that I left my love back there . . ."

"Yours . . . and mine," Quail said, sleepily.

"Yours . . . and mine, too. Be good, have some sympathy, go get 'em for us, really," Lard murmured.

"Yeah, Pancracio, ol' friend, it's gettin' cold 'round here. Go bring yourself the one-eyed María Antonia, she'll keep ya nice and warm," the Indian shouted from a distance.

Many burst out laughing, while Lard and Pancracio commenced their bout of insults and obscenities.

XX

"Villa's coming!"

The news spread as quick as lightning.

Ah, Villa! The magic name. The profile of a great man; the

unconquerable warrior who even from a distance exerts the fascination of a great boa.

"Our Mexican Napoleon!"[1] Luis Cervantes exclaims.

"Yes, 'the Aztec eagle who pierced the snake head of Victoriano Huerta with his steel beak,' as I proclaimed in a speech in Ciudad Juárez," Alberto Solís—Natera's assistant—says in something of an ironic tone.

The two were sitting at the counter in a tavern chasing back tall glasses of beer.

And as they ate and drank without stopping, the big hats—with their calloused, cowboy hands, wearing scarves around their necks and thick leather boots on their feet—spoke only of Villa and his troops.

The stories told by Natera's men left Macías's astonished and openmouthed.

"Oh, Villa! The battles of Ciudad Juárez, of Tierra Blanca, of Chihuahua, of Torreón!"[2]

But having seen and lived through the events was nothing compared to hearing the telling of Villa's formidable feats, in which acts of surprising magnanimity are immediately followed by the most bestial of deeds. Villa is the untamable master of the Sierra, the eternal victim of all governments, who pursue him as if he were an animal. Villa is the reincarnation of the old legend: the providential bandit blazing through the world with the bright torch of an ideal—to steal from the rich and give to the poor! And the poor carve out his legend, which time will be certain to adorn so it may live for generations to come.

"And I can tell ya for sure, my friend Montañés," one of Natera's men said, "that if General Villa is happy with ya, he'll give ya a hacienda. But if he's not . . . he'll send ya before the firing squad!"

"Ah, Villa's troops! All pure men from the north, dressed to kill, with Texan sombreros, brand new khaki suits, and four-dollar pair a' shoes from the U.S."

As Natera's men recounted all this, they looked at each other dejectedly, entirely aware that their own large palm-leaf sombreros were worn down by the sun and rain, and that their shirts and trousers were rags in tatters barely covering their dirty, lice-ridden bodies.

"Because no one goes hungry when they're with Villa. Their wagons are full of oxen, sheep, cows. Cars with clothes. Trains packed with equipment, supplies, and weapons. And enough food for everyone to eat till they're stuffed."

Then they spoke of Villa's aeroplanes.[3]

"Ah, the aeroplanes! When they're on the ground, and *landing* you're right next to 'em, you don't know what they are. *him* They look like canoes, like chalupa-shaped rafts. But when they start to go up, compadre, the sound they make is ear-piercing, it leaves you stunned. Then it's kind of like an automobile going real strong. Try to imagine a large bird, a very large bird, that looks all of a sudden like it's not even moving. And here's the best part: inside this metal bird, a gringo carries thousands of grenades. Just imagine what that's like! When it's time to fight, it's like feeding corn to the chickens, just droppin' fistful after fistful of lead on the enemy . . . And before long all that's left on the battlefield is a cemetery: dead over here, dead over there, dead every which way!"

When Anastasio Montañés asked his interlocutor if Natera's people had already fought side by side with Villa's, it came out that everything they knew about what they were recounting came by word of mouth, and that none of them had ever seen Villa's face.

"H'm . . . well, seems to me that man to man we're all the same . . . S'far as I'm concerned, nobody's more man than nobody else. To fight, all ya need to be is a little bit shameless. S'far as I'm concerned, I'm no soldier nor nothin' like that. But lookit here, just as ya see me standin' in these here rags, I can fight with the best of 'em . . . Ya don't believe me, do ya? Well, it's the truth, I don't need nothin' special to go out and fight . . ."

"I own ten yokes of oxen! Ya don't believe me?" Quail said behind Anastasio's back, laughing loudly as he mimicked him.

XXI

The deafening sound of rifle fire diminished and began to fade. Luis Cervantes got his courage to stick his head out of his hiding place, amid all the rubble, at the highest point of the hill.

He barely knew how he had gotten there. He was not certain at what point Demetrio and the men around him had disappeared. He had suddenly found himself alone. Then, seized by an avalanche of infantry, he was knocked off his saddle. He had been trampled, and when he had finally straightened up, a man on horseback had come by, grabbed him, and thrown him over the horse's rump. But shortly afterward the horse and the riders all hit the ground, and Luis Cervantes found himself in the middle of white clouds of gun smoke and whizzing bullets, not knowing where his own rifle or revolver were, nor what had happened. And the trench where he now found himself, protected by crumbling adobe, was the safest hiding place he had seen.

"Comrade!"

"Comrade!"

"My horse threw me and I was jumped upon by the enemy. They took me for dead and took my weapons . . . What was I to do?" a saddened Luis Cervantes explained.

"I was not thrown by anyone . . . I am here as a precaution . . . Know what I mean?"

Alberto Solís's mocking tone made Luis Cervantes blush.

"Oh, heavens!" Solís exclaimed. "Your leader is quite a fine man! What daring, what presence of mind! Not just me but many other well-traveled men were left gasping with astonishment."

Luis Cervantes, confused, did not know what to say.

"Ah! Were you not there? Bravo! You must have found a safe haven just in time! Listen, comrade. Come closer, let me tell you all about it. We were advancing over there, behind that summit. Note that on that side of the slope, near the foot of the hill, the only accessible route is the one we had in front of us. To the right the slope is extremely sharp, cut almost vertically, and any maneuvering in that direction is impossible. On the left it is even worse: the drop is so dangerous that one false step and you fall and roll and are shredded against the sharp edges of the stones. Well then. One section of Moya's brigade, we get down on the slope, our chests to the ground, set to attack the first trenches of the Federales. The bullets are whizzing by, passing just over our heads. The fighting has broken out everywhere. Then there is a moment when they stop firing on us. We thought that another group must be attacking them vigorously from the rear. So we get up and rush the trenches. Ah, comrade, you cannot imagine the scene at that point! Up and down the slope it is a veritable tapestry of corpses. The machine guns did all the work.[1] They literally swept us all away, leaving only a few of us able to escape. The generals were livid, and hesitated as to whether they should order a new charge with the reinforcements that had just arrived. And that was when Demetrio Macías, without waiting for anyone nor asking for any orders, yelled:

"'Charge! Up we go, muchachos! Let's get 'em!'

"'How barbaric,' I clamored, amazed.

"The other leaders, taken by surprise, did not utter a single word. Macías's horse climbed over the boulders as if it had the claws of an eagle instead of hoofs. 'Up we go, up we go!' his men yelled, following after him like cattle, men and beasts scaling up the rocks all as one. Only one young man lost his footing and fell to the abyss. The others reached the top of the hill in the briefest of instants, knocking down the fortifications and stabbing at the soldiers. Demetrio lassoed the machine guns, pulling at them as if they were wild bulls. Still, it could not have lasted, as they were vastly outnumbered. They would have been annihilated in less time than it had taken them to get there. But we took advantage of the temporary confusion, and with vertiginous speed we charged their positions and threw them off with utmost ease. Ah, your leader is such a beautiful soldier!"

From where they stood atop the hill, they had a clear view

of one side of the Cerro de la Bufa, its crest set against the sky like the plumed head of a lofty Aztec king. The steep slope to the side, six hundred meters in length, was littered with dead men, their hair in tangles, their clothes covered in dirt and blood. Among the heaps and piles of bodies, most of which were still warm, women in tatters went back and forth like starving coyotes, searching and stripping the corpses of their possessions.

Houses with large doors and many boarded-up windows shone in the bright sun amid the white smoke from all the gunfire and the black clouds rising from a few burning buildings. The streets seemed superimposed, as they wound in picturesque slopes, rising up to the surrounding hills. And above the graceful houses could be seen the slender columns of a grange and the towers and domes of the city churches.

"Ah, the beauty of the revolution, even at its most barbaric!" an emotional Solís declared. Then, in a soft voice and with a trace of melancholy, he added:

"Such a shame that what must come now shall not be quite as beautiful. We must wait a bit. Until there are no more combatants, until no shots are heard other than those of the masses surrendered to the delight of plundering. Until the psychology of our race can shine diaphanous, light as a drop of water, condensed into two words: theft, murder! What a disappointment it would be, my friend, if those of us who came with all our enthusiasm, with our very lives, to defeat a wretched assassin,[2] turn out to be the builders of an enormous pedestal upon which a hundred or two hundred thousand monsters of the same species might arise! A nation without ideals, a nation of tyrants! The shame of blood!"

Many fugitive Federales were climbing past, fleeing from soldiers wearing large palm-leaf sombreros and broad white trousers.

A bullet whizzed by.

Alberto Solís had been deep in thought after his last words, sitting with his arms crossed, but he was suddenly startled, and said:

"Comrade, these damned buzzing mosquitoes are certainly taking a liking to me. Shall we distance ourselves from here a bit?"

But Luis Cervantes's smile was so disdainful that an embarrassed Solís quietly sat down on a large rock.

Again he smiled as he let his gaze wander, following the spirals of smoke from the rifles and the clouds of dust from each demolished house and each collapsed roof. He thought he had found a symbol of the revolution in those clouds of smoke and dust rising fraternally, embracing each other, blending together and then dissipating into nothing.

"Ah!" he exclaimed suddenly. "That's it!"

He pointed toward the train station with his outstretched hand. The trains blowing furiously, hurling thick columns of smoke, the cars overflowing with people escaping at full steam.

He felt a small, dry blow to his abdomen and slipped off the rock, as if his legs had turned to jelly. He heard a buzzing in his ears . . . Then eternal darkness and silence . . .

PART 2

I

how some treat the revolution : as a game

Demetrio Macías prefers the clear tequila of Jalisco to bubbly champagne that fizzes under dim candlelight.

Men covered in dirt, smoke, and sweat, with kinky beards and wild manes of hair, dressed in filthy rags, gather around the tables of a tavern.

"I killed two colonels," exclaims a short, fat subject in a gruff, guttural voice, wearing a hat with galloon trim, a suede jacket, and a silk scarf around his neck. "They were so potbellied they couldn't even run. They stumbled over the rocks, they turned beet red, and their tongues hung out to here when they tried to climb the hill. 'Don't run so hard, little conservative mongrels,' I yelled at them. 'Stop running, I don't like scared chickens. Stop right there, you blockheads, I'm not gonna hurt ya. Stop right there, it's over!' Ha, ha, ha! They really fell for it, those . . . Bang, bang! One for each of those . . . And they were finally able to rest in peace!"

"I had one of those real big shots get away from me," a soldier with a blackened face said from a corner of the saloon between the wall and the counter, where he sat with his rifle between his outstretched legs. "Oh, he was covered in

gold, damn 'im! The braid on his epaulettes and his cape
sparkled. But what did I do? I'm such an ass that I let 'im go
by! He took out his handkerchief, gave me the password,
and I just stood there, my mouth wide open. But as soon as
he clears the corner, he turns back and starts shootin' and
shootin'! I waited until he finished shootin' off an entire
round of bullets . . . And there I go! Holy Mother of Jalpa,
don't let me miss this son of a . . . ! But nothin' doin', just
the sound of the gunfire and 'im makin' a break for it. He
had some horse! Flashed before my eyes like lightning. Another poor fool comin' up the same street paid for it instead.
Made 'im do some flip!"

They constantly interrupt each other, seizing the words
from each other's mouths. And while they recount their adventures with macho fervor, women with olive-colored skin,
bright eyes, and ivory teeth—with revolvers at their waists,
cartridge belts across their chests, and large palm-leaf sombreros on their heads—roam from one group to the other
like street dogs.

A very coarse-featured and very-dark complexioned
woman, with rouge-smeared cheeks, jumps up on the bar of
the cantina, near Demetrio's table. He turns to face her and
meets a lascivious pair of eyes under a small forehead, between two strands of unkempt hair.

The door swings wide open and Anastasio Montañés,
Pancracio, Quail, and the Indian come through. They stop
in their tracks, openmouthed and astonished.

Anastasio shouts out, surprised, and rushes forward to
greet the short, fat *chorro*[1] wearing the hat with the galloon
trim and the silk scarf around his neck. They are old friends
who have just recognized each other. They embrace so
tightly that their faces start to turn purple.

"Compadre Demetrio, allow me to introduce Towhead
Margarito[2] to ya. A true friend! Oh, how I love this towhead! Ya'll see, ya'll get to know 'im, compadre . . . He's
quite a man! Remember, Towhead, the Escobedo penitentiary, down in Jalisco? One year together!"

Demetrio, who remained silent and taciturn in the middle of all the commotion, stretched his hand out to him. Without removing the cigar from his mouth, he muttered between his teeth:

"Delighted . . ."

"Are you Demetrio Macías, then?" asked the young woman all of a sudden, bursting in from atop the bar, swinging her legs and tapping Demetrio on the back with her coarse leather shoes.

"At your service," he replied, barely turning his head around.

Indifferent, she continued moving her uncovered legs, showing off her blue stockings.

"Hey, War Paint![3] You, around here? Come, get down from there, come have a drink," Towhead Margarito said to her.

The young woman immediately accepted the invitation and impudently made room for herself to sit facing Demetrio.

"So ya're the famous Demetrio Macías, the one who shone so brightly in Zacatecas?" War Paint asked him.

Demetrio nodded yes, just as Towhead Margarito let out a burst of joyous laughter and said: "You devil, War Paint, you are a quick one! Already trying your hand at a general!"

Not understanding him, Demetrio raised his eyes toward the young woman. They faced each other like two strange dogs sniffing around with distrust. Unable to sustain War Paint's furiously provocative gaze, Demetrio lowered his eyes.

From where they sat at their tables, some of Natera's officers began to make obscene remarks toward War Paint.

But without paying them any heed whatsoever, she said, "General Natera is gonna give ya a little eagle. Come on, put it there!" And she stretched her hand out to Demetrio and shook his with the strength of a man.

Flattered by the congratulatory remarks that started raining in upon him, Demetrio ordered champagne.

"No, I cannot have wine right now, I am not so well," Towhead Margarito said to the waiter; "just bring me some ice water."

"I want something for dinner, as long as it's not chilies or frijoles, bring me whatever you have," Pancracio ordered.

Officers kept coming in, and the restaurant slowly filled up. It was teeming with stars and bars on hats of all shapes and forms, large silk scarves at the neck, rings with thick diamonds, and heavy gold watch chains.

"Listen here, waiter," Towhead Margarito yelled, "I asked you for ice water . . . And I am not asking for any handouts, either. Look at this stack of bills. I can buy you and . . . every woman in your house, even your wife, do you understand? I do not care if you ran out, or why you ran out. You can figure out where to get more. I am warning you, I have quite a temper! I am telling you that I do not want any explanations, just bring me some ice water . . . Are you bringing me some or not? Oh, no? Well, then . . ."

The waiter falls, knocked down by a loud slap across his face.

"That is how I am, General Macías. Notice how I do not have a single hair left on my face? Want to know why? Well, it is because of my fiery temper. When I do not have anyone to let it out on, I pull out my hairs until my anger dies down. I swear, my General, that if I did not do this, I would die from the pent-up rage!"

"It's very bad to swallow your own rage," affirms very seriously a man wearing a straw sombrero as if it were the roof of a hut. "I killed a woman in Torreón[4] 'cause she didn't want to sell me a plate of enchiladas. There was a big ol' argument about 'em. I didn't get to eat what I wanted, but at least I calmed down."

"I killed a shopkeeper in Parral[5] 'cause he slipped two bills from Huerta[6] in with the change," said another man with a small star, his blackened, calloused fingers glittering with jewels.

"I killed a guy in Chihuahua[7] 'cause I always ran into 'im at the same table at the same time whenever I'd go in to eat lunch . . . He really annoyed me! What do ya want?"

"H'm! I killed . . ."

THEME (handwritten)

The theme is inexhaustible.

Near dawn, when the restaurant is full of joy and spittle—when the dark, ashen-faced women from the north mix with the young girls from the suburbs wearing garish makeup—Demetrio takes out his stone-encrusted gold pocket watch and asks Anastasio Montañés to tell him the time.

Anastasio stares at the face of the watch, then sticks his head out a window and, looking up at the starry sky, says:

"The Seven Sisters[8] are hangin' way down, compadre. Dawn's not far off now."

Outside the restaurant, the drunken yelling and the loud laughter and singing are ceaseless. Soldiers on horseback ride wildly by, cracking their whips on the sidewalks. Rifle and pistol shots can be heard throughout the city.

Demetrio and War Paint stagger down the middle of the street, arm in arm, toward the hotel.

II

"What a bunch of animals!" War Paint exclaimed, laughing loudly. "Where d'ya say ya was from? The days when soldiers stay in inns are over. Where're ya from? As soon as ya get anywhere all ya have to do is choose the house that best suits ya and ya go and take it, ya don't ask no one. If not, who the hell was the revolution for? For city dandies? No, we're gonna be the dandies now, don't ya know? Let's see, Pancracio, hand me your machete for a minute . . . Damn these rich folk! They keep everythin' under lock and key . . ."

She dug the tip of the steel blade into the slit between a drawer and its desktop. Then, using the handle to get leverage, she broke the lock and yanked the splintered top off the desk.

Anastasio Montañés, Pancracio, and War Paint sank their hands into the pile of letters, stamps, photographs, and other papers scattered all over the rug.

Pancracio expressed his anger at not finding anything to

Pancracio always follows orders (handwritten)

his liking by kicking into the air, with the point of his leather sandal, a framed portrait, the glass covering of which shattered in the middle of the room.

Cursing, they withdrew their empty hands from among all the papers.

But the tireless War Paint continued breaking the locks off drawer after drawer, leaving no corner unexamined.

They did not notice when a small box, covered in gray velvet, rolled silently away, ending up at the feet of Luis Cervantes.

At this point, Luis Cervantes—who had been looking on with an air of deep indifference, while Demetrio seemed to sleep, spread out on the rug—pulled the small box in with the tip of his shoe without saying anything. Then he bent over, scratched his ankle, and deftly picked it up.

He was astonished: it contained two diamonds, of very pure glint, set in a filigree mount. He quickly hid it in his pocket.

When Demetrio awoke, Luis Cervantes said to him:

"General, look at this mess the boys have made. Would it not be preferable to avoid all this?"

"No, *curro*. Poor fellows! It's the only pleasure they have left after stickin' their necks out in combat."

"Yes, General, but at least not here. Look at all this, this kind of action ruins our good name and, what is even worse, it ruins the reputation of our cause . . ."

Demetrio fixed his eaglet eyes on Luis Cervantes. He tapped his teeth with his fingernails, and said: "Don't get all worked up now . . . Listen, don't come tellin' me about all that! We all know that what's yours is yours, and what's mine's mine. You got that little box, okay then. I got the pocket watch, and tha's that."

And the two, very much in harmony now, showed each other their "advance."

Meanwhile, War Paint and her companions were searching through the rest of the house.

Quail walked into a room where he found a twelve-year-old girl, her forehead and arms already marked with copper-colored stains. Astounded, both remained still as they contemplated the piles of books on the carpet, tables, and chairs, the broken mirrors pulled off the walls, and the furniture and knickknacks in pieces. Quail sucked in his breath and stared at his prey with avid eyes.

Outside, in a corner of the patio, amid the suffocating smoke, Lard was roasting small ears of corn, feeding the fire with books and papers that went up in bright flames.

"Ah!" Quail suddenly shouted, "look at what I found me! Perfect saddle blankets for my mare!"

And with one swift motion he yanked down a plush curtain, which came crashing down, with curtain rod and everything, and landed on the finely carved headpiece of a large chair.

"Look at this . . . look at all these bare, naked women!" exclaimed Quail's young girl, amused and entertained by the pages of a deluxe volume of the *Divine Comedy*. "I like this one, this one I'm takin' for myself." And she began to tear out the engravings that most drew her attention.

Demetrio got up and took a seat next to Luis Cervantes. He ordered a beer, handed a bottle to his secretary, and drank his down in one long gulp. Then, drowsy again, he half-closed his eyes and fell back asleep.

"Listen," a man in the doorway said to Pancracio. "At what time could I speak to the general?"

"You can't talk to 'im at any time. He woke up with a hangover," Pancracio answered. "What do ya want?"

"I want to buy one of those books that they're burnin' over there."

"I can sell those to ya myself."

"How much you want for them?"

A perplexed Pancracio knitted his eyebrows: "Well, let's see. The ones with pictures in 'em, those are five cents each. The others . . . I'll give ya the whole lot of 'em for free if ya buy all the books with pictures."

The man came back for the books with a bushel basket.

"Demetrio, ol' man, Demetrio, wake up already," War Paint yelled. "Stop sleepin' like a fat pig! Look who's here!

It's Towhead Margarito! Don't ya know what kind of man this towhead is?"

"General Macías, I have come to tell you that I have the greatest admiration for you, that I have a very strong will, and that I like your manner of doing things very much. Therefore, if you are not opposed to it, I would like to transfer into your brigade."

"What's your rank?" Demetrio asked.

"First captain, General."

"Come on, then. Come with me and I'll make you a major."

Towhead Margarito was a short, chubby man, with handlebar mustaches and very evil blue eyes that disappeared between his cheeks and his forehead when he laughed. Formerly a waiter in the Delmónico restaurant in Chihuahua, he now proudly wore three brass bars, the insignia of his rank in the northern division.

Towhead Margarito poured praise upon Demetrio and his men, and this was all it took for a box of beer to be emptied in a flash.

All of a sudden War Paint appeared in the middle of the room, parading about in a splendid silk gown with very fine lace.

"The only thing missing are the stockings!" Towhead Margarito exclaimed, splitting his sides with laughter.

Quail's girl also burst out laughing loudly.

But War Paint remained unperturbed. She shrugged off the comments, plopped down on the rug, and kicked off her white satin slippers, waving with evident pleasure her previously entombed bare toes in the air. Then she said: "Hey, you, Pancracio! Go get me a pair of blue stockings from my 'advances.'"

The room was getting more and more crowded with new friends and old battle comrades. Becoming lively again, Demetrio was starting to recount in minute detail some of his most notable feats of arms.

"Hey, what's that noise?" he asked all of a sudden, surprised by the tuning of strings and brass instruments in the patio of the house.

"General Demetrio Macías," Luis Cervantes said solemnly. "It is a banquet that your old friends and comrades offer you in celebration of the feat of arms of Zacatecas and your well-deserved promotion to general."

III

"General Macías, allow me to present to you my future wife," Luis Cervantes announced emphatically, leading a girl of unusual beauty into the dining room.

Everyone turned toward her, and she opened her large blue eyes, bewildered.

She was perhaps fourteen years of age. Her skin was ruddy and smooth as a rose petal, her hair was blond, and her eyes had a trace of malignant curiosity and much vague childish fear in them.

Luis Cervantes noticed that Demetrio fixed his bird-of-prey eyes on her, and felt satisfied.

They made room for her to sit between Towhead Margarito and Luis Cervantes, facing Demetrio.

There were numerous bottles of tequila among the fine glasses, porcelain, and flower vases.

The Indian came in, sweating and cursing, carrying a box of beers on his shoulder.

"You all don't know what this towhead is all about yet," War Paint said, noticing that the man she was referring to did not once take his eyes from Luis Cervantes's fiancée. "He's real smart, all right, and I never seen a quicker man in the whole wide world."

She shot him an insinuating glance, then added:

"Tha's why I can't stand to look at 'im, any which way!"

The orchestra broke into a splendid bullfighting march.

The soldiers bellowed with joy.

"This menudo[1] is wonderful, General! I swear I have never had one prepared as well as this in my entire life," Towhead Margarito said, as he reminisced about the Delmónico in Chihuahua.

"You really like it, Towhead?" Demetrio replied. "In that case, have 'em keep servin' it until ya're all full."

"Tha's exactly how I like it," Anastasio Montañés agreed. "Tha's how it's good. I like a good stew until . . . until . . . I'm so stuffed I'm burpin' it out."

Sounds of slurping and big swigs followed. Everyone drank copiously.

At the end, Luis Cervantes lifted a glass of champagne and stood up:

"My esteemed General . . ."

"H'm!" War Paint interrupted. "Here comes the speech, and that always really bores me. I'm off to the corral instead, since there's no more to eat anyhow."

Luis Cervantes presented Demetrio Macías a black cloth escutcheon with a small brass eagle. And he accompanied it with a toast that no one understood but which everyone applauded vigorously.

Demetrio grabbed the insignia representing his new rank. Then, with his face very flushed, his eyes sparkling, and his teeth gleaming, he said, full of ingenuousness: "And what am I supposed to do with this buzzard?"

Anastasio Montañés stood up and said, trembling, "My dear compadre, I don't need to tell ya . . ."

Entire minutes passed by, but the damned words would not come to compadre Anastasio. His face turned red, making the beads of sweat on his dirt-encrusted forehead glow like pearls.

"Well . . . I don't need to tell ya . . . that you know that I'm your compadre . . ."

And as everyone had applauded Luis Cervantes when he had finished, Anastasio gave the sign for everyone to applaud him as well, by clapping very seriously himself.

But it turned out just fine, for his awkwardness served as an incentive to the others, and Lard and Quail also made toasts.

It was about to be the Indian's turn when War Paint appeared, shouting out in jubilation. Clicking her tongue, she was trying to lead a beautiful jet-black mare into the dining room.

"My 'advance'! My 'advance'!" she exclaimed, patting the fiery animal's arched neck.

The mare resisted coming through the door, but a pull on its halter and a whip snapped on its croup made it enter, spiritedly and clamorously.

The enthralled soldiers stared at the rich catch with ill-concealed envy.

"I don't know how this damned War Paint does it, but she always beats us to the best 'advances'!" Towhead Margarito exclaimed. "That is how it has been with her since she joined us in Tierra Blanca."[2]

"Hey, you, Pancracio, go fetch me a bundle of alfalfa for my mare," War Paint ordered curtly.

Then she handed the rope off to a soldier.

Once again all the cups and glasses were filled. Some of the men were beginning to tilt back, close their eyes, and nod off, while most still yelled loudly and joyfully.

In the middle of it all, Luis Cervantes's girl, who had spilled all her wine on a handkerchief, looked around everywhere with her big blue eyes full of astonishment.

"Muchachos," Towhead Margarito shouted in a sharp, guttural voice, standing and making himself heard over the din, "I am tired of living, I feel like killing myself now. I am sick and tired of War Paint already . . . And this little cherub from heaven will not even deign to look at me . . ."

Luis Cervantes noticed that the last few words were directed at his girlfriend, and with much surprise he realized that the foot he felt between those of the girl's was not Demetrio's but Towhead Margarito's. Indignation burned in his chest.

"Look here, muchachos," Towhead continued, holding up his revolver. "I am going to shoot myself right in the middle of my forehead!"

And he aimed at the large mirror at the end of the room, where he could see his entire body reflected.

"Do not budge, War Paint!"

The mirror shattered in long, sharp pieces. The bullet had whizzed past War Paint's head, but she had not even flinched.

IV

In the afternoon, Luis Cervantes awoke, rubbed his eyes, and sat up. He had been lying on the hard ground, among the flowerpots of the orchard. Near him Anastasio Montañés, Pancracio, and Quail breathed loudly, deep asleep.

He felt his lips cracked and his nose swollen and dried out, saw that he had blood on his hands and on his shirt, and all of a sudden recalled what had happened. He quickly got up and walked toward a room, pushed at the door several times, but was unable to open it. He stood indecisively for a few moments, uncertain what to do.

Because it was all true; he was certain that he had not dreamed it. He had gotten up from the dining room table with his girl and had led her to the room. But before they closed the door behind them, Demetrio had hurried after them, staggering drunk. Then War Paint had followed Demetrio, and they started to struggle. Demetrio—his eyes burning like red-hot coals, with clear threads of spittle on his coarse lips—had avidly sought out the girl, while War Paint forcefully shoved him, trying to hold him back.

"What're ya doing? What d'ya think ya're doin'?" Demetrio was howling, exasperated.

War Paint stuck one of her legs between his, took leverage, and threw Demetrio lengthwise, outside the room.

He got up, furious.

"Help! Help! She's tryin' to kill me!"

War Paint vigorously grabbed Demetrio's wrist and redirected the barrel of his pistol.

The bullet shot into the bricks. War Paint continued to bellow. Anastasio Montañés came up behind Demetrio and disarmed him.

Macías turned around, his eyes wild like those of a bull in the middle of the plaza. Luis Cervantes, Anastasio, Lard, and many others surrounded him.

"Damn ya! You've taken my gun! As if I needed a weapon to deal with the likes of ya!"

And swinging his arms, he began to throw quick, vigorous punches, knocking anyone he could reach to the brick floor.

And then? Luis Cervantes could not recall what had happened next. Everyone must have ended up receiving quite a beating and passing out. And his girlfriend, afraid of so many animals, must have taken the wise prevention of locking herself up somewhere.

"Perhaps that room over there connects with the hall and I can get in that way," he thought.

His footsteps woke up War Paint, who was sleeping near Demetrio on the carpet, at the feet of a love seat piled with alfalfa and corn, which the black mare was calmly eating.

"What d'ya want?" the young woman asked. "Oh, yeah. I know what ya want, ya lowlife! Listen, I locked up your girlfriend 'cause I couldn't hold back this dog Demetrio no more. Grab the key, it's over there on the table."

Luis Cervantes searched throughout the house in vain.

"Let's see, *curro,* tell me what the story is with that girl of yours."

A very nervous Luis Cervantes continued looking for the key.

"Don't get all anxious, man, I'll give it ya. But tell me . . . I really like all those kind of stories. That little *curra* is just like ya . . . She's not country folk like us."

"I have nothing to tell . . . She is my girlfriend and that is that."

"Ha, ha, ha! Your girlfriend and tha's . . . no! Listen, *curro.* I'm way ahead of ya. I have hard fangs where ya have baby teeth. Lard and the Indian grabbed her outta her house; that much I know already . . . But ya must'a given 'em somethin' for her . . . some gold-plated cuff links . . . Some miraculous little stamp of Our Lord of la Villita . . . Am I right, *curro?* I know these people exist, I just know it! The thing is to find one of 'em! Isn't that right?"

War Paint got up to give him the key and was very surprised when she did not find it either.

She stood for a long while, thinking.

All of a sudden she ran at full speed toward the door of

the next room and looked through the keyhole. She remained still until her eyesight became accustomed to the dark. Directly, and without looking away, she muttered:

"Oh, Towhead . . . Son of a . . . ! Step right up, *curro*!"

And she moved out of the way, laughing loudly.

"Like I said, never in my life have I seen a smoother man than that one in there!"

The next morning, War Paint waited to feed her horse until she spotted Towhead coming out of the room.

"You young thing, you! Go on, go on home! These men are liable to kill ya! Go on, run!"

And she draped Lard's louse-ridden blanket over the girl with the large blue eyes and the virgin expression on her face, as she was wearing only stockings and a nightgown. Then she took her by the hand, led her out to the street, and exclaimed:

"Good Lord! Now, I really . . . Oh, how I love that Towhead!"

V

Demetrio's men cross the Sierra like the colts that neigh and frolic at the first thunders of May.

"To Moyahua, muchachos!"

"To the land of Demetrio Macías."

"To the land of the cacique Don Mónico!"

The landscape clears, the sun peeks out from behind a scarlet girdle over the diaphanous sky.

Gradually the cordilleras emerge like variegated monsters with sharply angled vertebrae: hills like the heads of colossal Aztec idols—with giant faces, grimacing frightfully and grotesquely—which alternately make one smile or leave one with a vague sense of terror, something akin to a mysterious foreboding.

At the head of the troop rides Demetrio Macías with his general staff: Colonel Anastasio Montañés, Lieutenant

Colonel Pancracio, and Majors Luis Cervantes and Tow-head Margarito.

They are followed, in the second row, by War Paint and Venancio, who is wooing her in a very refined manner, reciting the despairing verses of Antonio Plaza.[1]

Four abreast, they began to enter Moyahua, blowing their clarions as the rays of the sun skirted the low outlying walls surrounding the houses of the town.

The roosters crowed a deafening sound, and the dogs barked loudly, in warning. But there was no sign of human life anywhere.

War Paint snapped her black mare with her whip and in one leap was riding next to Demetrio. She wore a silk dress and long gold earrings with pride and joy; the pale blue of the fabric accentuated the olive tint of her face and the coppery stains of the damage. With open legs, she had her skirt pulled up to her knees to reveal her worn-out stockings, full of holes. She carried a revolver at her chest and a cartridge belt crossed over the front of her saddle.

Demetrio was also in full dress: a gallooned hat, suede pants with silver buckles, and a sheepskin jacket embroidered with gold thread.

The forcing open of doors began. The soldiers, already spread out through the town, were gathering weapons and mounts from everywhere in the surrounding area.

"We're gonna stop by Don Mónico's house today," Demetrio announced in a serious tone, as he dismounted and handed his horse's reins to a soldier. "We're gonna have lunch with Don Mónico . . . an old friend who really cares for me . . ."

His general staff smile a sinister smile.

Dragging their spurs loudly along the sidewalks, they head toward a large, pretentious house, which could only be the residence of the cacique.

"It's shut tight," Anastasio Montañés said, pushing at the door with all his might.

"But it's about to open right up," Pancracio replied, quickly bringing his rifle to the mouth of the lock.

"No, no," Demetrio said. "Knock first."

Three blows with the butt of the rifle, and another three, but no one answers. Pancracio curses and no longer follows his orders. He fires, the lock snaps, and the door opens.

They see the bottoms of skirts and the legs of children, all scattering to hide inside the house.

"Wine, I want wine! Bring me wine right here!" Demetrio demands with an imperious voice, pounding his fist hard and repeatedly on the table.

"Have a seat, friends."

A woman slowly emerges, then another, and another. From between their black skirts the heads of frightened children peek out. One of the women, trembling, walks toward a cupboard, takes out glasses and bottles, and serves wine.

"What weapons do you have here?" Demetrio asks, harshly.

"Weapons?" the woman answers, her tongue thick as a rag. "What weapons do you want us to have? We are but a handful of decent women, by ourselves."

"Ah, by yourselves, huh? And Don Mónico?"

"He is not here, señores . . . We just rent his house . . . We only know Don Mónico by name."

Demetrio orders that the place be sacked.

"No señores, please . . . We will give you everything we have, and we will bring it to you ourselves. But, for the love of God, do not harm us. We are decent girls, all on our own!"

"And the little urchins?" Pancracio asks, brutally. "Did they sprout like vegetables out in the garden?"

The women quickly disappear and at once return with a cracked rifle, covered with dust and spiderwebs, and a pistol with rusty, broken springs.

Demetrio smiles.

"Okay, let's see the money then . . ."

"Money? What money do you expect us to have? We are but a few poor girls living by ourselves."

They turn their imploring eyes toward the soldiers closest to them; but then they shut their eyes, horrified. For they have seen the executioner crucifying Our Lord Jesus Christ along the Way of the Cross at the parish church! They have seen Pancracio!

Demetrio gives the order for the sacking to begin.

The women all rush off again and return immediately, this time with a moth-eaten purse and a few bills, of the kind issued by Huerta.[2]

Demetrio smiles. And now, without further ado, he has his people enter the house.

The mob rushes in like hungry dogs that can smell their prey, running over the women who had sought to block the entrance with their own bodies. Some faint and fall, others flee; the children scream.

Pancracio begins to break the lock of a large dresser. But before he can do so, the doors open and a man jumps out with a rifle in his hands.

"Don Mónico!" they exclaim, surprised.

"Dear sir, Demetrio! Do not hurt me! Do not harm me! I am your friend, Don Demetrio!"

Demetrio Macías laughs sarcastically and asks him if he always welcomes his friends with a rifle in his hands.

Don Mónico, confused and stunned, throws himself at Macías's feet, hugs his knees, kisses his feet: "My wife! My children! My dear friend Don Demetrio!"

With his hand shaking, Demetrio puts his revolver back into its holster at his waist.

A painful silhouette has flashed across his memory. A woman with a child in her arms, climbing over the boulders of the Sierra at midnight, by moonlight . . . A burning house . . .

"Let's go! Everyone, outside!" he shouts, somberly.

His general staff obeys him. Don Mónico and the women kiss his hands and cry gratefully.

Out in the street, a happy and loud mob is waiting for the general's permission to plunder the house of the cacique.

"I know exactly where the money's hidden, but I'm not tellin'," a young man says, holding a basket under his arm.

"H'm, I know, I know!" replies an old woman, carrying a

hirsute sack to gather "what God wishes her to have." "It's in the attic. There's a bunch of things in there, and among all the things there's a small trunk with shells painted on it. Tha's where all the good stuff is!"

"Tha's not true," a man says. "They're not so stupid that they're gonna store their money like that. The way I see it, they've hidden it in a dry well, buried in a leather knapsack."

The people in the crowd stir about, some with ropes to carry their bundles, others with washtubs. The women stretch out their aprons or the ends of their shawls, figuring out how much they will be able to carry. Everyone, giving thanks to His Divine Majesty, waits for their good portion of the plundering.

When Demetrio announces that he will not allow anything to happen and orders that everyone retire, the townspeople obey him, their heads hanging low as they slowly disperse. But among the soldiers there is a muffled rumbling of disapproval, and none of them leave their places.

An irritated Demetrio repeats that they are to retire.

A young fellow, from among the last to have been recruited—his head clouded by a few drinks—laughs and advances toward the door, altogether ignoring the order.

But before he can cross the threshold, a gunshot makes him instantly collapse, like a bull stabbed by the matador's dagger.

His pistol smoking in his hands, Demetrio waits immobile while the soldiers retire.

"Burn the house down," he orders Luis Cervantes when they reach their quarters.

Luis Cervantes, with rare solicitude and without passing the order on to anyone else, makes sure to carry it out himself.

When a couple of hours later the small town plaza was full of black smoke, and enormous flames lapped up from Don Mónico's house, no one understood the general's strange behavior.

VI

They had taken lodgings in a large, somber house, a property that also belonged to the cacique of Moyahua.

Their predecessors had already left their energetic mark on the estate: outside in the patio, which was transformed into a dung heap; on the walls, stripped down to the raw adobe; on the floors, cracked under the hooves of their animals; and in the orchard, turned into a pile of wilted leaves and dry branches. From the moment one entered, broken-off furniture legs and chair backs and bottoms were scattered about, and everything was covered with dirt and slop.

At ten at night, a very bored Luis Cervantes yawned and said good night to Towhead Margarito and War Paint, who were drinking nonstop on a bench in the plaza.

He walked back to the barracks. The only room with furniture in it was the main hall. When he came in, Demetrio—lying down on the floor, staring at the ceiling with blank eyes—stopped counting the beams up above and turned his head:

"Is that you, *curro*? What's going on? Come on in, have a seat."

Luis Cervantes went first to trim the candle. Then he pulled up a chair, the back of which was missing and the wicker seat of which had been replaced with burlap. The legs of the chair screeched, and War Paint's dark mare snorted and stirred in the shadows, where its elegant curve could be seen, with its round, smooth croup.

Luis Cervantes sank down into the seat and said:

"General, I have come to give you an account of the commission . . . Here you have . . ."

"But *curro,* man . . . that's not what I wanted! Moyahua is almost like my own land. You might say that that's why I'm here!" Demetrio replied, looking at the heavy bag of coins that Luis was holding out to him.

Cervantes left his seat to come sit on his haunches next to

Demetrio. He spread a serape out on the floor and emptied out the large sack of coins, which glowed like golden embers, onto it.

"First of all, General, only you and I know about this. And furthermore, you know that when the sun is shining one must open the windows wide. Today it shines bright in our faces; but what of tomorrow? One must always think ahead. A stray bullet, a horse that suddenly bolts, even a ridiculous little cold . . . and one is left with a widow and orphans in misery! The government? Ha, ha, ha! You try going to Carranza, to Villa, or to any of the other main leaders and talking to them about your family. The best you can hope for from them is a swift kick in the you-know-what. And they do the right thing, General. We did not rise up in arms so that some Carranza or some Villa could become president of the republic. We fight on behalf of the sacred rights of the people, stomped upon by the evil cacique. And just as Villa, or Carranza, or anyone else from the government, does not come here to ask for our approval to pay themselves for the services they are rendering the motherland, neither do we need to ask anyone for license for our actions."

Demetrio sat halfway up, grabbed a bottle from the floor near his head, and tilted it back. Then, he puffed out his cheeks and spat out a mouthful far away from himself.

"Man, you talk a lot, *curro*!"

Luis suddenly felt light-headed. The beer he had jugged seemed to inflame the fermentation of the trash heap where they were sitting: a tapestry of orange and banana peels, meaty watermelon rinds, stringy mango pits, and sugarcane husks, all mixed together with tamale and enchilada wrappers, and all wet with excrement.

Demetrio's calloused fingers went back and forth over the shining coins, counting them over and over again.

Recovered from his dizziness, Luis Cervantes took out a small Falliéres phosphate box and poured out many pendants, rings, earrings, brooches, and other valuable jewels from it.

"Listen, General. If this uproar is to continue, as it would appear that it will, if the revolution does not end, we already have enough to go abroad and live it up for a good while."

Demetrio shook his head no.

"Wouldn't you do that? What are we staying for, then? What cause would we be defending now?" Luis Cervantes asked.

"That's something that I just can't explain, *curro*. I just feel that it wouldn't be manly . . ." Demetrio replied.

"Take your pick, General," Luis Cervantes said, showing him all the jewels spread out before him.

"Keep it all for yourself. Really, *curro* . . . You know, I really don't care for money at all! Want me to tell you the truth? As long as I have enough to drink, and as long as I have me a little gal to keep me warm, I'm the happiest man in the world."

"Ha, ha ha! You crack me up, General! In that case, why do you put up with that snake War Paint, then?"

"Man, *curro*, I am sick of her, but that's how I am. I can't bring myself to tell her. I'm not brave enough to send her to . . . But that's how I am, that's my temperament. Listen, when I like a woman, I get so tongue-tied, that if she doesn't start things up . . . I don't do nothin'." And he sighed. "There's that Camila, you know, the girl from the little rancho. The girl's not the prettiest, but if you only knew how I dream of her . . ."

"The day you wish it, we are off to get her for you, General."

Demetrio's eyes shimmered avidly.

"I swear that I will do it right, General . . ."

"Really, *curro*? Listen, if you do this favor for me, you can have the pocket watch with the gold chain and everything, since you like it so much."

Luis Cervantes's eyes glowed. He gathered the phosphate box, filled it again, stood up, and said, smiling: "I will see you tomorrow, General. Good night to you."

VII

"What do I know? I don't know any more about it than you do. The General told me: 'Quail, saddle up your horse and my black mare. You're going with the *curro* on an errand for me.' And tha's what happened: we left here at noon and reached the little rancho 'round nightfall. One-eyed María Antonia put us up for the night. Says, 'How ya doin', Pancracio.' As soon as day breaks the *curro* wakes me up and says: 'Quail, Quail, saddle the horses. Leave me my horse and ride the general's mare back to Moyahua. I'll catch up with you in a little bit.' And the sun was already high above us when he reached me, with Camila on the seat with 'im. He helped her dismount and we put her up on the black mare."

"Okay, but what about her, what was the expression on her face?" one of the men asked.

"H'm, well, she was so happy she wouldn't stop talkin'!"

"And what about the *curro*?"

"Quiet as always. Like he always is."

"I believe," Venancio opined, very seriously, "that if Camila woke up in Demetrio's bed today, it must have just been a mistake. We drank quite a bit . . . remember! All the alcohol went to our heads and everyone lost track of what they were doing."

"It wasn't no alcohol goin' to no one's head! This was some kind of arrangement between the *curro* and the general."

"Of course! As far as I'm concerned, that *curro* is nothin' but a . . ."

"I do not like to speak about friends behind their back," Towhead Margarito said. "But I can tell you that of the two girlfriends of his that I have met, one was for . . . me, and the other was for the general . . ."

And everyone broke out in laughter.

Once War Paint realized exactly what had occurred, she consoled Camila very tenderly: "Poor little thing, tell me all about it, what happened to ya?"

Camila's eyes were swollen from so much crying.

"He lied to me, he lied! He came to the rancho and said: 'Camila, I've come back just for you. Won't you come with me?' H'm, and ya tell me if I didn't wanna go with 'im! Do I love 'im? I more than love 'im! I was so sick just thinkin' about 'im! When the sun would come up I didn't even wanna go grind the corn. When my mamma would call me to lunch, I'd chew the tortilla till it tasted like paste and I couldn't swallow it at all. And now it really hurts so bad!"

And she began to cry again, covering her mouth and nose with the end of her rebozo to drown her sobs.

"Listen, I'm gonna get ya outta this mess. Don't be silly, don't cry no more. Don't think about the *curro* no more. D'ya know what that *curro* is? Honestly! I'm tellin' ya tha's the only reason that the general has 'im round! What a fool! Okay, do ya wanna go back home?"

"The Virgin of Jalpa protect me! My mamma would beat me to death!"

"She won't do nothin'. This is what we'll do. The troops have to head out any moment now. When Demetrio tells ya to get ready to go, ya tell 'im that ya're sore and achy all over, that ya feel like someone's beaten ya, and ya stretch and yawn all the time. Then ya touch your forehead and say: 'I'm burnin' up.' Then I tell Demetrio to go on ahead and leave the two of us, that I'll stay behind to take care of ya, and that we'll catch up once ya're better. But what we'll do is that I'll take ya home, sound and safe."

VIII

The sun had already gone down, and the sad grayness of its old streets and the frightful silence of its still dwellings— closed at a very early hour—were settling over the small town, when Luis Cervantes arrived at Primitivo López's general store and interrupted a party that showed much promise. Demetrio was getting drunk there with his old comrades. The bar was packed to the gunnels. Demetrio,

War Paint, and Towhead Margarito had left their horses
outside, but the other officers had forced their way in with
their mounts and everything. Gallooned hats with colossal
concave brims were constantly coming and going; the horses'
croups turned this way and that, as the animals ceaselessly
adjusted their elegant heads, with their large black eyes, trembling nostrils, and small ears. And the horses' snorting could
be heard in the middle of the infernal din of the drunkards,
as well as the rough scraping of their hooves on the floor and
an occasional short, nervous neighing.

When Luis Cervantes arrived, a trivial story was being recounted. A townsman, with a small, bloody hole in his forehead, was lying face up in the middle of the road. The
various opinions, which at first had been quite divided, were
now coming together under a very just observation by Towhead Margarito. That poor devil lying very much dead was
the sacristan of the church. But the fool! It had all been his
fault. Whoever would think, señor, of wearing a pair of
trousers, a jacket, and a cap? Pancracio cannot stand seeing
a city dandy like that in front of him!

Eight musicians playing wind instruments—their faces
round and red like the sun, their eyes bulging out of their or-
bits—who have been blowing their lungs out since dawn,
stop playing at the orders of Cervantes.

"Dear General," Luis Cervantes said, making his way
through the mounted officers. "An urgent message has just
arrived. You have been ordered to leave immediately and go
after the Orozquistas."[1]

All the faces, at first darkened for a moment, now shone
with joy.

"We are going to Jalisco, muchachos!" Towhead Margarito shouted, pounding his hand loudly on the counter.

"Get ready, my dear Jalisco girls, I'm comin' for ya!"
Quail shouted, wringing his sombrero.

Everything was cheer and rejoicing. In the excitement of
drunkenness, Demetrio's friends offered to join his ranks.
Demetrio was so happy he could barely speak. "Ah, we're
gonna fight the Orozquistas! Finally we get to have it out

with real men! We can stop killin' Federales that are as easy to kill as rabbits and turkeys!"

"If I could catch Pascual Orozco alive," Towhead Margarito said, "I would scrape the bottom of his feet off and make him walk for twenty-four hours through the Sierra . . ."

"What, is he the one who killed Señor Madero?"[2] the Indian asked.

"No," Towhead replied, solemnly. "But he slapped me once when I was a waiter at the Delmónico in Chihuahua."

"The black mare's for Camila," Demetrio ordered Pancracio, who was already saddling the horses.

"Camila can't go," War Paint said quickly.

"Who asked for your opinion?" Demetrio replied, harshly.

"Isn't it true, Camila, that ya woke up sore and achy all over and that ya feel all feverish now?"

"Well I . . . well I . . . I'll do whatever Don Demetrio says."

"Ah, don't be a fool! Tell 'im ya're not goin', tell 'im ya're not goin'," War Paint whispered anxiously into her ear.

"The thing is I'm startin' to like 'im somewhat, can ya believe it?" Camila answered, also in a very soft voice.

War Paint turned purple and her cheeks burned red, but she said nothing. Instead, she walked off toward her mare, which Towhead Margarito was saddling for her.

IX

The whirlwind of dust, extending for a good stretch down the road, was abruptly broken by a dispersed, violent mass of men and horses—as puffed-out chests, unruly manes, flaring nostrils, ovoid and impetuous eyes, flying hooves, and legs stiffened from galloping, rode briskly through. The men with bronze faces, ivory teeth, and burning eyes brandished their rifles or slung them across the front of their saddles.

Bringing up the rearguard, trotting along, were Demetrio and Camila. She was still trembling, her lips dry and pale; he, in a bad mood because of how inane their move had been. There had been no Orozquistas, nor any battle even. Just a few dispersed Federales and a poor devil of a priest with about a hundred believers, all gathered under the archaic banner of "Religion and Order." The priest was left dangling from a mesquite tree, while the surrounding field was littered with the dead, all with a small red insignia sewn to their chests that read: "Stop! The Sacred Heart of Jesus is with me!"

"Truth is, I've already more than paid myself all my back pay," Quail said, showing off the gold watches and rings he had taken from the parish house.

"This kind of fightin' is really worth it," Lard exclaimed, intermingling obscenities after each sentence. "At least ya know why ya're riskin' your hide!"

In the same hand in which he held the horse's reins, he clutched a shiny ornament he had torn off one of the holy statues in the church.

When Quail, who was quite an expert in these matters, greedily examined Lard's "advance," he let out a grand burst of laughter:

"Your ornament is made out of tin!"

"Why are ya draggin' that piece of trash with ya?" Pancracio asked Towhead Margarito. One of the last to arrive, he had a prisoner with him.

"Do you want to know why? Because I have never seen the expression on the face of a man up close when a rope is tied tight around his neck."

The prisoner was a very fat individual, and his breathing was labored. His face was beet red, his eyes bloodshot, and his forehead dripping sweat. They had his wrists tied and kept him walking.

"Anastasio, lend me your rope; my halter is breaking with this pig's weight. No, don't; now that I think about it, I do not need it. My Federale friend, I am going to kill you right now; you have suffered long enough. Look, the mesquite trees are still quite a ways away, and there is not even a telegraph post around here to hang you."

Towhead Margarito took out his pistol, put the barrel of

the gun on the prisoner's left temple, and immediately cocked back the trigger.

The Federale turned white as a corpse; his face stretched out and his glassy eyes shattered. His chest was heaving wildly, his entire body shaking as if overcome by a strong current.

Towhead Margarito kept his pistol in that position for several eternal seconds. During this time, his eyes glowed in a strange fashion, and his plump face, with its burning cheeks, lit up with a feeling of supreme voluptuousness.

"No, my Federale friend!" he said, slowly pulling back his weapon and returning it to its holster. "I do not want to kill you yet. You are going to go on as my orderly. You will see whether my heart is that evil!"

And he winked maliciously to everyone around.

The prisoner had gone mad. The only thing he did was make swallowing sounds, but his mouth and throat were completely dry.

Camila, who had remained back a ways, spurred her horse and reached Demetrio: "Ah, that Margarito, he's such a bad man! If ya'd only seen what he's been doin' with a prisoner!"

She proceeded to tell him what she had just witnessed.

Demetrio knit his brows but did not say anything in reply.

War Paint called Camila away.

"Hey, you, what kinda gossip are ya spreadin' to Demetrio? I love Towhead Margarito more than anybody in the whole wide world. Just so you know! And now I've told ya . . . Whatever ya have against 'im, it's against me, too. Consider yourself warned!"

Camila, very frightened, hurried back to Demetrio.

X

The troop made camp on a plain, near three small, solitary houses lined up in a row, their white walls contrasting against the purple ring of the horizon. Demetrio and Camila went toward them.

Inside the corral, a man wearing a simple white shirt and trousers was standing, avidly puffing at a cornhusk cigarette. Near him, sitting on a stone slab, another man was shelling corn, rubbing husks together between his two hands and frequently shaking one of his legs—which was withered and dried out and had something like a goat's hoof on its end— to shoo away the chickens.

"Hurry up, Pifanio," said the man who was standing. "The sun has already set and you haven't brought down the water for the animals yet."

A horse neighed outside, and both men looked up, startled.

Demetrio and Camila were looking at them from behind the thatch of the corral fence.

"I'm just lookin' for lodgings for me and my woman," Demetrio said, reassuringly.

As soon as he explained that he was the leader of an army division that was going to spend the night nearby, the owner of the place—the man who had been standing up—anxiously asked them to come in. He ran to fetch a large tub of water and a broom, and immediately began to sweep and water down the best corner of the hut, so as to decently lodge such distinguished guests.

"Go on, Pifanio. Unsaddle the horses of the señor and the señora."

The man who had been shelling corn stood up, with much difficulty. He wore rags for a shirt and vest, and scraps for pants, their seams torn all the way down; and he had enormous calluses protruding from his waist.

As he walked his step marked a grotesque rhythm.

"Wait, friend, you don't look like you should be workin'!" Demetrio exclaimed, stopping him from unsaddling the horses.

"Poor man," the owner shouted from inside the hut. "He doesn't have much strength! But you should see how good he earns his salary! He starts workin' the minute God wakes up! And the sun's already set . . . and look at 'im, he's still goin'!"

Demetrio went out with Camila to take a look around the encampment. The plain, with its golden fallows, shorn even of bushes, stretched out, immense in its desolation. The three large ash trees in front of the small houses seemed like a veritable miracle, with their dark green tops, round and undulating, and their rich foliage drooping down to kiss the ground.

"I don't know what it is about this place, but it just makes me feel so sad!" Demetrio said.

"Yes," Camila replied. "I feel the same."

At the banks of a small creek, Pifanio was heaving roughly from the rope of a small water pump. An enormous pot spilled over a large pile of fresh herbs, and the crystal spray from the stream sparkled by the last light of the afternoon. A skinny cow, a wrecked horse, and a burro were drinking loudly.

Demetrio recognized the crippled laborer and asked him:

"How much do you make a day, my friend?"

"Sixteen cents, señor."

He was a small, weak man, with scrofula scars, straight blond hair, and light blue eyes. He cursed the owner of the place, the ranch, and his dogged luck.

"You really earn your pay, my son," Demetrio interrupted him, speaking gently. "You swear and swear, but still you work and work."

And turning to Camila, he said: "There's always others worse off than those of us from the Sierra, right?"

"Yes," Camila replied.

And they continued walking.

The valley was covered in darkness, and the stars came out.

Demetrio embraced Camila lovingly around the waist, and who knows what words he murmured into her ear.

"Yes," she replied, weakly.

Because she was already "startin' to like 'im somewhat."

Demetrio slept poorly. He left the house at a very early hour.

"Something's going to happen to me," he thought.

It was a quiet dawn, filled with subtle happiness: a thrush chirping timidly in the ash tree, the animals in the corral rummaging through the refuse in the mud, and the pig grunting off his sleep. The orange hue of the sun appeared on the horizon, and the last little star went out.

Demetrio walked slowly toward the encampment.

He was thinking about his yoke and plow back home, about his two brand-new dark oxen, which he had worked for only two years, and about his two acres of well-fertilized land. He saw his young wife's outline faithfully reproduced in his mind: those sweet curves—infinitely yielding for the husband, but proud with indomitable energy for all strangers. But when he tried to conjure up the image of his son, all his attempts were in vain; he had forgotten what he looked like.

He reached the encampment. The soldiers slept, stretched out in the furrows of the field, alongside the horses—which were also lying down, their heads fallen, their eyes closed.

"The animals are pretty worn out, compadre Anastasio. It would be good to stay and rest at least for a day."

"Oh, compadre Demetrio! You don't know how much I miss the Sierra already! If ya only knew . . . I bet ya don't believe me? But nothin' that I find 'round here . . . It's all sad and grim! God knows how much I miss it all!"

"How many hours is it from here to Limón?"

"It's not a matter of hours. It's a long three-day ride, compadre Demetrio."

"If ya only knew! I really wanna see my wife!"

Not long after this War Paint went off to find Camila, and said to her:

"Oh, wow! I just heard Demetrio is about to leave ya. He just told me, he told me 'imself. He's gonna bring his wife here, he really is. And she's real purty, real light-skinned! Ya should see her features! But if ya don't wanna leave, ya can stay and be of some service: they have a kid and ya can take care of 'im . . ."

When Demetrio returned, a crying Camila told him everything War Paint had said.

"Don't pay any heed to that madwoman. It's lies, all
lies . . ."

And as Demetrio did not go to Limón, or recall his wife
again, Camila was very happy, while War Paint turned into
a scorpion.

XI

They set out for Tepatitlán[1] before dawn. Dispersed along
the main road and the surrounding fields, their silhouettes
undulated gently to the monotonous, measured gait of their
horses, then faded into the pearl hue of the waning moon
bathing the entire valley.

The barking of dogs could be heard in the distance.

"Today, by noon, we'll reach Tepatitlán. Tomorrow we'll
be in Cuquío.[2] And then . . . the Sierra," Demetrio said.

"Would it not be advisable, General," Luis Cervantes
commented in Demetrio's ear, "to stop first by Aguascalientes?"[3]

"What would we do there?"

"We are running out of money . . ."

"What! Forty thousand pesos in eight days?"

"Just this week, we recruited nearly five hundred men,
and we spent it all on advances and bonuses," Luis Cervantes replied, very softly.

"No. We're going straight to the Sierra. After that, we'll
see . . ."

"Yeah, to the Sierra!" many around them exclaimed.

"The Sierra! The Sierra! There's no place like the Sierra."

The plains continued to weigh heavily upon their chests.
They spoke deliriously of the Sierra, full of enthusiasm,
thinking of her as the longed-after lover whom they had not
seen in a long time.

Dawn broke. Soon afterward, to the east, a reddish dust
cloud arose and formed an immense curtain of burning
purple.

Luis Cervantes reined in his horse and waited for Quail.

"So what is it going to be, Quail?"

"Like I told you before: two hundred just for the watch . . ."

"No. I will buy the whole stack from you: watches, rings, and all the other jewels. How much for the whole thing?"

Quail wavered, and his face turned pale. Then he quickly said:

"Let's say two thousand bills for everythin'."

But Luis Cervantes gave himself away. His eyes shone with such evident greed that Quail backpedaled, exclaiming at once:

"No, no, no, I'm not sellin' nothin' . . . Just the watch, tha's all, and I'll sell it 'cause I owe those two hundred pesos to Pancracio, who beat me again last night."

Luis Cervantes took out four crisp, brand-new "two-faced" bills[4] and placed them in Quail's hands.

"Really, though," he said. "What I am interested in is the whole lot. No one is going to give you more than me for everything."

They were feeling the sun above them when Lard suddenly yelled:

"Hey, Towhead Margarito, your orderly is ready to burst. Says he can't walk no more."

The prisoner had let himself fall, exhausted, in the middle of the road.

"Quiet!" Towhead Margarito exclaimed, taking a few steps back. "So you are tired already, my friend? Poor little thing! I am going to buy a glass case to keep you in a corner of my house, like the Baby Jesus. But first we must reach the town, so I will help you get there."

And he took out his saber and hit the poor wretch repeatedly with it.

"Let us have the rope, Pancracio," he said then, his eyes shining strangely.

But as Quail pointed out to him that the Federale was no longer moving, he laughed loudly, and said:

"I am such an animal! Just when I had trained him to survive without eating!"

"This is it, we've arrived in Little Guadalajara," Venancio said, spotting the small, pleasant town of Tepatitlán, nestled gently into the hillside.

They entered full of joy. Smiling faces with beautiful black eyes looked out through the windows.

The schools were transformed into quarters, and Demetrio took up lodgings in the sacristy of an abandoned chapel.

Then the soldiers dispersed, as usual, in search of "advances," under the pretext of gathering weapons and horses.

In the afternoon, several from Demetrio's escort were lying about in the church atrium, scratching their bellies. A bare-chested Venancio was very seriously dedicating himself to delousing his shirt.

A man approached and peered over the wall, asking for permission to speak with the leader.

The soldiers looked up, but no one answered him.

"I'm a widower, señores. I have nine children and work all day to survive. Don't be mean with the poor!"

"If ya're lookin' for a woman, don't worry, ol' man," the Indian said, tallowing his feet with the end of a candle. "There's War Paint over there, we'll let ya have 'er for nothin' at all."

The man smiled bitterly.

"She's only got one fault, though," Pancracio added, lying on his back, looking up at the sky. "The moment she sees her man, she goes all crazy."

Everyone burst out laughing. But Venancio very seriously pointed toward the sacristy door for the townsman.

The man walked in, timidly, and told Demetrio his complaint. The soldiers had just "cleaned him out." They had taken everything, leaving him without a single grain of corn.

"Well, why'd ya let 'em?" Demetrio replied, lazily.

The man continued to insist, moaning and whining. Luis Cervantes got up, insolently, prepared to throw him out. But Camila intervened:

"Come on, Don Demetrio, don't ya be so mean too. Give 'em an order to give the man his corn back!"

Luis Cervantes had to obey. He jotted down a few sentences, and Demetrio added his scribble at the bottom.

"May God repay you for this, my girl! God will bless ya in his holy glory. Ten bushels of corn, just 'nough to eat this year," the man exclaimed, crying as he thanked them. And he took the paper and kissed all their hands.

XII

As they were getting closer to Cuquío, Anastasio Montañés approached Demetrio and said:

"Listen, compadre, I haven't even told ya yet . . . That Towhead Margarito is really somethin'! Do ya know what he did yesterday with that man who came to complain that we had taken all his corn for our horses? Well, the man took the order that ya gave 'im to the quarters. 'Yes, my friend,' Towhead said to 'im. 'Come on in, over here. It's only fair that you get your share back. Come in, come in. How many bushels did we steal? Yes, that's it, about fifteen, more or less . . . Or maybe twenty? Try to remember . . . You're a very poor man, you have lots of children to feed. Yes, that's what I said, about twenty, that must be it, over there . . . Come over here. I'm not going to give you fifteen, nor twenty. You just start counting. One, two, three . . . And when you've had enough, you just let me know, okay?' And he takes out his sword and starts beating 'im until the man's beggin' for mercy."

War Paint was laughing so hard she nearly fell off her horse.

And Camila, unable to hold back, said:

"Damn that old man, he's a bastard! No wonder I can't stand 'im!"

War Paint's expression changed at once.

"So ya're gonna go get all huffy about that?"

Camila, frightened, urged her mare forward.

War Paint stirruped hers at once and shot forward. Overtaking Camila, she grabbed the girl by the hair and undid her braid.

The pull made Camila's mare rear back, and the girl released the reins to get her hair out of her face. This made her lose her balance and fall off the horse, hitting her forehead against the stones.

Laughing uncontrollably, War Paint galloped off very agilely to catch the runaway mare.

"There ya go, *curro,* ya got yourself a new patient!" Pancracio said, when he saw Camila sitting on Demetrio's saddle along with Macías, her face covered in blood.

Luis Cervantes went forward presumptuously with his healing supplies. But Camila stopped crying, wiped her eyes, and said in a hushed voice:

"From you? Not even on my deathbed! I wouldn't take a drop of water from ya!"

In Cuquío, Demetrio received another order via courier.

"It says to head back to Tepatitlán again, General," Luis Cervantes said, scanning the communication quickly. "You will have to leave your people there, and head to Lagos,[1] to take the train to Aguascalientes."

There were heated complaints. Amid much grumbling, grunting, and whining, some from the Sierra swore that they would break off from the troops.

Camila cried all night long. The next day, in the morning, she asked Demetrio to give her license to return home.

"If ya don't like it no more!" Demetrio replied, gruffly.

"It's not that, Don Demetrio. I like ya, I like you plenty . . . But ya've seen what's going on . . . it's that woman!"

"Don't worry, I'll get rid of her this very day . . . I've already thought it all out."

Camila stopped crying.

Everyone was already saddling their horses when Demetrio approached War Paint and whispered softly to her:

"You're not goin' any farther with us."

"What're ya sayin'?" she asked, not understanding him.

"That you're stayin' here, or you're goin' off to wherever ya want, but you're not comin' with us."

"What're ya sayin'?" She gasped. "Ya mean ya're gettin'

rid of me? Ha, ha, ha! What the . . . ? I suppose ya believe everythin' that girl says!"

Then War Paint proceeded to insult Camila, Demetrio, Luis Cervantes—and everyone else she could think of—with such energy and originality that the troops ended up hearing obscenities and insolences they had not even suspected might exist.

Demetrio waited patiently for quite a while. But since she showed no sign of stopping whatsoever, he said very calmly to a soldier:

"Throw this drunk woman outta here."

"Margarito! My dear towhead! Come defend me from these . . . ! Come on, dear towhead of my heart! Come show 'em that ya're a real man, and that they're nothin' but a bunch of sons of . . . !"

And she kicked and screamed and made obscene gestures as she yelled all this.

Towhead Margarito came forward. He had recently awoken. His blue eyes could barely be seen behind his swollen eyelids, and his voice was hoarse. When he found out what had happened, he approached War Paint and said very seriously to her:

"Yes, I think it is a good idea, it is more than time for you to go! We have all had it up to here with you!"

War Paint's face turned to stone. She tried to speak, but her muscles were frozen stiff.

The soldiers were all laughing, thoroughly enjoying themselves. Camila, very frightened, held her breath.

War Paint looked carefully all around her. Then everything happened in the blink of an eye: she reached down, unsheathed a sharp bright blade from inside her stockings, and jumped on Camila.

A shrill cry and a body collapses, spurting blood everywhere.

"Kill her," Demetrio screamed, mad with rage.

Two soldiers went toward War Paint. But she wielded her knife and did not allow them to touch her.

"Not you, damned nothings! You kill me yourself, Demetrio," she said as she went forward, handed him her weapon, stuck out her chest, and dropped her arms to her sides.

Demetrio raised the bloodstained knife high in the air. But his eyes clouded over; he wavered and took a step back.

Then, in a choked, hoarse voice, he shouted:

"Get outta here! Outta here now!"

No one dared to stop her.

She walked away slowly, somberly.

The silence and the overall astonishment were finally broken by the sharp, guttural voice of Towhead Margarito.

"Thank goodness! I am finally rid of that pest!"

XIII

> Someone stabbed me with a knife,
> deep into my body
> not knowing why,
> nor do I know why . . .
> He must've known why,
> but I never knew . . .
> And from that mortal wound
> much blood did I lose,
> not knowing why,
> nor do I know why . . .
> He must've known why,
> but I never knew . . .

With his head drooped down and his hands resting across his saddle, Demetrio kept humming the tune softly, in a woeful tone.

Then he would grow quiet, and remain silent and dejected for long minutes.

"As soon as we get to Lagos I will help you get rid of that melancholy, you will see, General. There are many pretty girls there for us to choose from," Towhead Margarito said to him.

"The only thing I want right now is to get drunk," Demetrio replied.

And he took his distance from them again, spurring his horse forward, as if he wished to abandon himself entirely to his sadness.

After many hours of slow riding, he called for Luis Cervantes.

"Listen, *curro*, now that I think of it, what in the hell am I goin' to Aguascalientes for?"

"To cast your vote, General, for the provisional president of the republic."[1]

"The provisional president? So, then, should I . . . should it be Carranza? Truth is, I don't understand nothin' about this politics business . . ."

They arrived in Lagos. Towhead bet that he could make Demetrio laugh in earnest that evening.

Dragging his spurs, with his goatskin breeches drooping below his waist, Demetrio entered El Cosmopolita with Luis Cervantes, Towhead Margarito, and his orderlies.

"Why are you running away, *curros*? We are not going to eat you!" Towhead exclaimed.

The townsfolk, startled just as they were trying to escape, stopped dead in their tracks. Some, pretending they were simply going about their business, returned to their tables and continued drinking and talking; others hesitated and then went forward to offer their respects to the general and his staff.

"General! Such an honor to meet you! Major!"

"That is better! That is how I like my friends, decent and refined," Towhead Margarito said.

"Let's do it, muchachos," he added, jovially drawing his pistol. "Here go your firecrackers, let's see your best dance moves."

A bullet ricocheted off the cement floor and whizzed through the legs of the tables and of the well-dressed young men sitting around them, making everyone jump up, as frightened as a lady who has just seen a mouse crawl under her skirts.

Pale, they smile to appropriately celebrate the major. Demetrio barely parts his lips, while the rest of the staff erupts in uncontrollable laughter.

"Towhead," Quail observes. "Looks like that one over there who's leavin' got stung by a bee, look at the way he's limpin'."

Towhead, completely indifferent to what Quail has just said, not even turning around to look at the wounded man, states enthusiastically that he can hit a bottle of tequila at the drop of a hat from a distance of thirty steps.

"Let's see, friend, stand up," he says to the waiter of the cantina. Then he leads him by the hand to the front of the hotel patio and puts a full tequila bottle on his head.

The poor, frightened wretch resists and tries to escape, but Towhead draws his pistol and aims.

"Stay in your place . . . you idiot! Or I will really give you a nice little warm one."

Towhead walks back to the opposite wall, raises his weapon, and aims.

The bottle shatters into pieces, soaking the pale-as-a-corpse youth's head with tequila.

"Now we are talking!" he exclaims, and runs to the cantina for a new bottle, which he once again places on the young man's head.

He goes back to his spot, turns suddenly in place, draws, and fires.

Except this time he has shot off an ear instead of the bottle.

And, doubled over, holding his stomach from laughing so hard, he says to the young man:

"Here you go, boy, take these bills. It is really nothing! You can cure that with a little bit of arnica and alcohol . . ."

After drinking many spirits and beers, Demetrio speaks.

"Pay up, Towhead . . . I'm leavin' now . . ."

"I do not have anything left, General. But do not worry about it . . . How much do we owe you, friend?"

"A hundred and eighty pesos, señor," the bartender replies amiably.

Towhead quickly jumps up on the counter and swings both of his arms about, knocking over all the cups, glasses, and bottles.

"Go on and send the bill to your Papi Villa, okay?"

"Listen, friend," he asks—staggering drunk—of a small, properly dressed subject who is closing the door of a tailor's shop. "Where can we find the girls around here?"

The man who has been asked this steps down politely from a stool to let them pass. Towhead stops and looks at him with impertinence and curiosity.

"Listen, friend, you certainly are small and pretty! What do you mean no? Are you calling me a liar, then? Okay then, that is better . . . Do you know how to do the midget dance? What do you mean you do not know? I am sure you know it! I have seen you dancing with the circus! I am sure that you know it, and that you know it really good! We will see now!"

Towhead draws his pistol and starts firing at the tailor's feet. The very fat, small man jumps with each shot.

"See, I told you that you knew how to do the midget dance!"

Throwing his arms around his friends, he has himself led to the red light district, marking each step along the way by shooting at the corner streetlights and at the doors and the houses. Demetrio lets him go and returns to the hotel, singing under his breath:

> *Someone stabbed me with a knife,*
> *deep into my body*
> *not knowing why,*
> *nor do I know why . . .*

XIV

Cigar smoke, the pungent smell of sweat on dirty clothes, alcohol breath, and the breathing of a multitude, more packed than a car full of pigs. Most wear Texan sombreros adorned with gold galloon, and khaki colors.

"Gentlemen, a well-dressed gentleman stole my suitcase in the station of Silao[1] . . . I had my life savings in there. I don't even have 'nough left to feed my child," a sharp, whiny voice laments, but is quickly drowned out by the din in the train car.

"What is that old lady saying?" Towhead Margarito asked, entering in search of a seat.

"Somethin' about a suitcase . . . and a well-dressed boy . . ." replied Pancracio, who had already found the laps of some peasants on which to sit.

Demetrio and the others forced their way in, throwing elbows to make room for themselves. And since the poor men who were holding Pancracio up decided that they preferred to abandon their seats and continue on their feet, Demetrio and Luis Cervantes took them, with pleasure.

A woman with a child in her arms, who had been riding standing up since Irapuato,[2] suddenly fainted. A peasant rushed forward to catch the baby. But no one else paid any heed: a few women traveling with the soldiers occupied two or three seats each with their luggage, dogs, cats, and parrots. And the men in Texan sombreros, in fact, got a good laugh at the plump thighs and limp breasts of the woman who had fainted.

"Gentlemen, a well-dressed man stole my suitcase in the station of Silao . . . I had my life savings in there. I don't even have 'nough left to feed my child."

The old woman speaks quickly, and immediately sighs and sobs. Her jittery eyes look every which way. And she collects a bill here, and another farther down. They shower money on her. She completes a collection and moves forward a few seats:

"Gentlemen, a well-dressed man stole my suitcase in the station of Silao . . ."

The effect of her words is certain and predictable.

A well-dressed man! A well-dressed man who steals a suitcase! It's unspeakable! It's enough to awaken a feeling of general indignation. Oh, it's too bad that the well-dressed man is not on hand so that at the very least each of the generals in the train could have a shot at him!

"Because there's nothing that makes me madder than a thieving *curro*," one man says, full of dignity.

"Stealin' from a poor old lady!"

"Stealin' from a poor, defenseless woman!"

And they all express the tenderness in their hearts in words and deeds: an insult for the thief and a five-peso bill for the victim.

"I will tell you, as far as I am concerned, I do not think that it is wrong to kill, because when you kill, it is always out of anger. But stealing?" exclaims Towhead Margarito.

Everyone seems to agree with such serious reasoning. But after a brief silence and a few moments of reflection, a colonel ventures to speak his mind:

"Truth is that everything has its time and place. No one truth is more true than any other, is it now? God's honest truth is that I've stolen . . . and I'd venture to say that everyone in this here train has done the same as well . . ."

"H'm, if you'd only seen the sewing machines that I stole in Mexico City!" exclaimed one major, enthusiastically. "I made more than five hundred pesos from 'em, sellin' 'em for fifty cents each."

"In Zacatecas I stole some horses that were so fine, I said to myself: 'After this you're all set, Pascual Mata. You won't have nothin' to worry about in all the days left in your life,'" said a toothless, white-haired captain. "Problem was that General Limón took a likin' to my horses, and he stole 'em from me."

"Okay, okay! Why deny it, then! I too have stolen," Towhead Margarito agreed. "But let my compatriots here say if I have accumulated any capital. The thing is, whatever I make, I spend it all on my friends. I would rather go on a drinking binge with my friends than send one penny to the women back home . . ."

The subject of "I stole," although it may seem inexhaustible, eventually peters out, and decks of cards are brought out and spread out on every bench, attracting the generals and the officers like mosquitoes to the light.

The sudden changes of fortune that accompany games of chance absorb everyone's attention, and the environment heats up even further. It smells of barracks, prisons, brothels, and even of pigsties.

And coming from the next car now, above the general din, can be heard:

"Gentlemen, a well-dressed man stole my suitcase . . ."

The streets of Aguascalientes had become a veritable trash heap. The men in khaki swarmed about like bees at the mouth of their hive, packing into the restaurants, the eating houses, and the taverns, and around the tables full of hotch-potch and the outdoor food stands, where piles of filthy cheese were stacked next to pans of rancid pork rinds.

The smell of fried food made Demetrio and his companions hungry. They pushed their way into one of the eating houses, where an unkempt, ugly old woman served them earthenware plates of pork bones swimming in a clear chili broth, with three leathery, burnt tortillas. They paid two pesos each, and when they left Pancracio said that he was hungrier than when they had gone in.

"Now we're ready," Demetrio said, "to consult with General Natera."

They walked down a street toward the house occupied by the northern commander.

Their progress was blocked by an unruly, agitated crowd at a street intersection. A man lost in the multitude was imploring in a singsongy voice, with an unctuous tone, as if he were praying. They moved in closer to investigate. The man, wearing faded white shirt and trousers, kept on repeating: "All good Catholics who devoutly utter this prayer to Jesus Christ, who died on the cross for us, will be freed of storms, and of plagues, and of war, and of hunger . . ."

"This guy's sure got it right," Demetrio said, smiling.

The man waved a handful of papers in the air, saying:

"Fifty cents per prayer to Our Lord upon the Cross, fifty cents . . ."

Then he would disappear for a moment, only to reappear immediately with a snake tooth, a starfish, a fish skeleton. And with the same predicant voice, he would expound the medicinal properties and rare virtues of each item.

Quail, who had no faith in Venancio, asked the vendor to pull out one of his molars for him. Towhead Margarito purchased the black pit of a certain fruit that had the power to protect its owner from lightning or from any such "bad luck." And Anastasio Montañés bought a prayer to Our Lord upon the Cross, which he carefully folded and put with much piety under his shirt.

"As sure as there's a God, my friend, the ball just keeps on rolling! Now it's Villa against Carranza,"[3] Natera said.

And Demetrio, without replying, opened his eyes very wide as a way to ask for further explanation.

"It means," Natera insisted, "that the convention won't recognize Carranza as the leader of the constitutionalist army and is now going to elect a provisional president of the republic instead.[4] Do you understand, my friend?"

Demetrio nodded to indicate that he did.

"What do you think of that, my friend?" Natera asked.

Demetrio shrugged, and said:

"So it means, apparently, that we'll just keep on fightin'. Okay then, let's get to it. You know, General, that as far as I'm concerned, nothin' can hold me back."

"Good. So on which side are you going to fight?"[5]

A perplexed Demetrio buried his hands in his hair, scratched his head for a moment, and said:

"Look, don't ask me questions like that, I'm not a schoolboy here. This little eagle that I wear on my hat, you gave me that . . . So you know that all ya have to do is say: 'Demetrio, you do such and such,' and I'll do it, end of story!"

PART 3

I

EL PASO, TEXAS, MAY 16, 1915[1]

MY DEAR VENANCIO:

I am only now able to reply to your pleasant letter of January of this year, since my professional responsibilities have absorbed all my time. As you know, I graduated last December. I was sorry to hear of the fate of Pancracio and Lard; but I am not surprised that they stabbed and killed each other after a card game. Such a pity; they were truly brave! I am sorry from the bottom of my heart that I am unable to communicate with Towhead Margarito to extend to him my warmest congratulations; clearly the most noble and beautiful act of his life was his last one: to commit suicide!

I think it would be difficult, my friend Venancio, for you to obtain the medical degree that you so desire here in the United States, even if you have gathered enough gold and silver to purchase it. I hold you in high esteem, Venancio, and I believe that you are very much deserving of a better fate. Therefore, I have an idea that would be favorable to both of our interests, as well as to the just ambitions that you have for yourself to change your social status. If you and I were to become partners, we could start a very nice business. It is true that I do not currently have any funds saved up, as I have spent everything on my studies and my stay here. However, I count on something that is worth much more than money: my perfect knowledge of this town and of its needs, and of the businesses that can be safely launched here. We could open an all-Mexican restaurant, with you as the owner and both of us splitting the profits at the end of each month. And it would be something related to that which interests both of us so much: a change in your social sphere. I recall that you play the guitar quite well, and I believe it would be a simple matter—through my recommendations and your musical knowledge—to get you admitted as a member of the Salvation Army, a very respectable organization that would give you much character.

Do not hesitate, dear Venancio. Come, bring your funds, and in a very short time we can be rich. Please extend my warmest regards to the general, to Anastasio, and to my other friends there.

Your caring friend, *Luis Cervantes.*

Venancio finished reading the letter for the hundredth time and again repeated his comment with a sigh:

"That *curro* really knew how to pull the whole thing off!"

"'Cause the thing I just can't get my head around," Anastasio Montañés observed, "is the fact that we have to go on fightin'... Didn't we already defeat the federation?"[2]

Neither the general nor Venancio answered him. But his words continued to resonate in their rough minds like a hammer on the yoke of a plow.

Thoughtful, with their heads bowed, they climbed up the hillside on their mules, proceeding at their mounts' slow gait. Anastasio, restless and stubborn, took the same observation to other groups of soldiers, all of whom laughed at his candor. Because if one carries a rifle in one's hands, and the cartridge belts are filled with bullets, it is surely to fight.

Against whom? On whose side? No one has ever cared about that!

The endless wavering column of dust stretched out in either direction of the path, in an ant line of palm-leaf sombreros, filthy old khakis, mossy blankets, and the black swirling of the horses.

Everyone was hot and thirsty. Not a single water well, nor creek, nor even puddle had they encountered along the way. A fiery fume of vapor rose from the white, barren bottom of a ravine and quivered above the curled crests of the huisache trees and the fleshy light green stems of the nopal cacti. And as if to mock them, the flowers of the cacti opened out—some with cool, leafy, bright colors, others thorny and diaphanous.

At midday they came across a hovel clinging to the cliffs of the Sierra. A little later, three small houses scattered along the banks of a river of calcined sand. But everything was silent and abandoned. As the troops approached, people hurried to hide in the surrounding canyons.

Demetrio became indignant.

"Grab anyone you find hidin' or runnin' from us and bring 'em to me," he ordered his soldiers, in a harsh voice.

"What! What did he say?" Valderrama exclaimed, surprised. "To bring 'im men who live in the Sierra? These brave men, the ones who didn't act like the chickens who are now nesting in Zacatecas and Aguascalientes? Our own brothers, who weather all manner of storms, clinging to the rocks like moss itself? I protest! I protest!"

He spurred the side of his miserable nag and trotted up beside the general.

"The men who live in the Sierra," he said to him, with emphasis and solemnity, "are our own flesh and bone . . . 'Os ex ossibus meis et caro de carne mea.'[3] The men who live in the Sierra are made from the same substance as we are. Of this solid substance out of which heroes are made . . ."

And with a confidence as unexpected as it was courageous, he pounded his fist against the general's chest. Demetrio smiled benevolently.

Did Valderrama—a mad vagabond and a bit of a poet—
know what he was doing?

When the soldiers reached a rancho, they whirled raven-
ously into the surrounding houses and shacks, all of which
were empty. But they did not find a single stale tortilla, nor
one rotten chili, nor even a pinch of salt with which to flavor
the horrible taste of jerked meat. Their peaceful brothers,
the owners of the huts, would then come out of their hiding
places, some impassive with the stonelike impassivity of Aztec
idols, others with more human reactions. With a sordid
smile on their pale lips and beardless faces, they looked on
as the ferocious intruders, who just a month earlier would
have made their miserable, remote homes tremble with
fear, now emerge from the same small, poor houses—where
the stoves were cold and the water tanks dry—with their
heads bowed, humiliated like dogs kicked out of their own
homes.

But the general did not cancel his orders, and a small
group of soldiers brought him four well-bound fugitives.

II

"Why do you hide from us?" Demetrio asked the prisoners.

"We weren't hidin', General. We were just on our way."

"Where to?"

"To our own homes . . . In the name of God, to Durango."[1]

"Is this the road to Durango?"

"Peaceful men can't walk on the roads these days. You
know that, General."

"You're not peaceful men, you're deserters. Where're you
comin' from?" Demetrio asked, looking at them with a keen
eye.

The prisoners became confused and looked at each other,
perplexed, unable to come up with a quick answer.

"They're Carranzista scorpions,"[2] one of the soldiers said.

This comment brought the prisoners immediately back to their senses. The terrible enigma that had arisen from the beginning, with respect to this unknown army, had been completely dissipated.

"Us, Carranzistas?" one of them answered proudly. "We'd rather be pigs!"

"Truth is, we are deserters," another said. "We cut out from General Villa's troops on this side of the Celaya,[3] after the beatin' they gave us."

"General Villa, defeated? Ha, ha, ha!" The soldiers burst out laughing.

But Demetrio knitted his brow as if a very dark shadow had passed before his eyes.

"The son of a . . . with enough to defeat General Villa has not been born yet!" a veteran with a coppery face and a scar from forehead to chin exclaimed insolently.

Unfazed, one of the deserters looked firmly into his eyes, and said:

"I know you. When we took Torreón, you were fighting with General Urbina.[4] In Zacatecas you were already with Natera, and there you joined up with those from Jalisco . . . Am I right?"

The effect of these words was sudden and definitive. The prisoners were then allowed to give a detailed account of Villa's tremendous defeat in Celaya.[5]

Everyone listened to them in stupefied silence.

They lit fires to roast bull meat before resuming their march. While he was off searching for firewood among the huisache trees, Anastasio Montañés saw the close-cropped neck of Valderrama's nag in the distance, behind some boulders.

"Come on back now, you crazy fool, they didn't cook no stew after all . . . !" he shouted in his direction.

Because the romantic poet Valderrama always managed to keep a good distance for the entire day whenever they started talking about firing squads.

Valderrama heard Anastasio's voice from afar, and he

must have been convinced that the prisoners had been freed, because soon thereafter he was back near Venancio and Demetrio.

"Did you hear the news?" Venancio asked him, very seriously.

"I don't know anything."

"It's very grave! A disaster! Villa defeated in Celaya by Obregón. Carranza's winning everywhere. We're ruined!"

Valderrama's expression was solemn and disdainful, like that of an emperor, as he said:

"Villa? Obregón? Carranza? X . . . Y . . . Z! What do I care? I love the revolution like I love an erupting volcano! I love the volcano because it is a volcano and the revolution because it is the revolution! But the rocks that remain above or below after the cataclysm, what are they to me?"

And since the image of a white bottle of tequila was reflected on his forehead with the glare of the midday sun, he turned on his heels and rushed off toward the bearer of such a tremendous wonder, his soul brimming with joy

"I like that crazy fool," Demetrio said, smiling. "Because sometimes he says some things that make ya think."

The march was resumed, and the overall uneasiness translated into a lugubrious silence. Quietly but unfailingly they carried with them the news of the catastrophe: a defeated Villa was a fallen god. And fallen gods cease being gods, or anything else for that matter.

When Quail spoke, his words were a faithful transcription of the general feeling:

"Well, this time it's really true, muchachos . . . Now it's every man for himself!"

III

The next small town, like all groups of houses, haciendas, and ranchos, had emptied out and everyone had fled to Zacatecas and Aguascalientes.

It was thus a small miracle that one of the officers had

found a barrel of tequila. Thorough care and much secrecy were undertaken so that the troops would be ready to leave the next morning, at dawn, under the leadership of Anastasio Montañés and Venancio. When Demetrio awoke to the sound of music, his general staff—now composed primarily of young ex-Federales—conveyed to him the news of the discovery. Quail, articulating the thoughts of his colleagues, spoke as if he were declaring a maxim:

"The times are bad and we have to take advantage of whatever we find, because 'if there are days when the duck swims peacefully, there are others when he doesn't even have a drop of water to drink.'"

The string musicians played all day long, and solemn toasts were made to the barrel. But Demetrio remained very sad, constantly muttering under his breath "not knowing why, nor do I know why" as if it were a refrain.

Cockfights were organized for the afternoon. Demetrio and his chief officers sat in the shade, under the cover of the municipal arcades, in front of an enormous plaza with overgrown weeds, a decrepit old stand, and a handful of abandoned adobe houses.

"Valderrama!" Demetrio called, looking wearily away from the ring. "Come sing me 'The Gravedigger.'"

But Valderrama did not hear him, because instead of paying attention to the cockfight, he was watching the sun setting behind the hills and reciting an impassioned soliloquy. In an emphatic voice, with solemn gestures, he was saying:

"My Lord, my Lord, it is good that You have brought us here! I shall raise three tents: one for You, another for Moses, and another for Elijah."

"Valderrama!" Demetrio yelled again. "Sing me 'The Gravedigger.'"

"Hey, ya crazy fool, the general is callin' ya," an officer closer to him said.

Valderrama, with his eternally complacent smile on his lips, finally came and asked the musicians for a guitar.

"Silence!" the gamblers yelled.

Valderrama finished tuning the instrument. Just then,

Quail and the Indian threw a pair of cocks—armed with long, very sharp blades—into the ring of sand. One was wine red, glimmering with beautiful obsidian streaks; the other, sandy yellow, with iridescent feathers like fiery copper scales.

The fight was swift and almost as fierce as a human battle. The cocks lunged at each other as if shot out of a spring. Their feathers standing on end, their necks arched, their eyes like corals, their combs erect, their legs sticking straight out—for a moment they did not even touch the ground, as their plumage, beaks, and claws were lost in a dizzying whirl. Then the wine-red cock broke away and was thrust outside the line of the ring, its legs sticking straight up. His vermilion eyes became extinguished as his leathery lids slowly closed, his tangled feathers quivering as the animal convulsed in a pool of blood.

Valderrama, who could not repress an expression of violent indignation, started strumming his guitar. His anger dissipated with the first solemn sounds of the song. His shining eyes gleamed with the light of madness. Letting his gaze wander over the square, the ruined stand, and the old houses, with the hills behind him and the burning sky above, he began to sing.

He was able to put so much soul in his voice, and such feeling in the chords of his old guitar, that when he finished Demetrio had turned his face away so that no one would see his eyes.

But Valderrama embraced him and held him tightly with that sudden closeness that he always assumed at some point toward everyone he met. And he said into Demetrio's ear:

"Drink them up! Those tears are very beautiful!"

Demetrio asked for the bottle and handed it to Valderrama.

Valderrama avidly drank half of it down, almost in one gulp. Then he turned to everyone around him and exclaimed dramatically, in a declamatory tone, with tears in his eyes:

"Behold how the great wonders of the revolution are resolved in a single tear!"

And he proceeded to speak madly, but completely mad, to the dusty weeds, the decrepit stand, the gray houses, the tall hills, and the incommensurable sky.

IV

Juchipila could be seen in the distance. It was bathed in white sunlight in the middle of green foliage, at the foot of a tall, impressive hill that folded around the town like a turban.

A few soldiers looked at the towers of Juchipila and sighed sadly. Their march through the canyons was now the march of a blind man without a guide. They could already feel the bitterness of exodus.

"Is that town Juchipila?" Valderrama asked.

Valderrama, in the first stages of the first drunkenness of the day, had been counting the crosses they had seen by the side of roads and paths, put up on the rugged, stony slopes, in uneven creek beds, and along the banks of the rivers. Crosses made with recently varnished black wood, crosses made with two sticks of wood hammered together, crosses made with a pile of stones, crosses painted with cal on demolished walls, extremely humble crosses drawn with charcoal on the side of boulders. The trail of blood of the first revolutionaries of 1910, murdered by the government.[1]

When they are within sight of Juchipila, Valderrama gets off his nag, kneels down, leans over, and gravely kisses the ground.

The other soldiers pass by him without stopping. Some laugh at the madman, while others joke and jest.

Without hearing anyone, Valderrama utters his solemn prayer:

"Juchipila, crib of the revolution of 1910,[2] blessed land, land watered with the blood of martyrs, with the blood of dreamers . . . of the only good men!"

"Because they didn't have time to be bad," an ex-Federale riding by brutally completes the sentence.

Valderrama stops talking, thinks for a moment, knits his

brow, and lets out a loud laugh that echoes through the hills. Then he remounts and hurries after the officer to ask for some of his tequila.

Maimed, crippled, rheumatic, and consumptive soldiers speak poorly of Demetrio. Men just off their mammas' laps are given tin stripes to wear on their sombreros and made officers before they even know how to handle a rifle—while the veteran who has taken fire in a hundred battles, and is now incapacitated for any kind of work, the veteran who started off as a common soldier, is a common soldier still.

And the few officers who are left, old comrades of Macías's, are also indignant because the ranks of the general staff have been filled with insignificant, perfumed, spruced-up dandies with capital.

"But the worst thing of all," Venancio says, "is that we're getting filled with ex-Federales."

Anastasio himself, who usually finds everything that his compadre Demetrio does to be right, now agrees with the general dissatisfaction, and exclaims:

"Listen, comrades, I always say what's on my mind . . . and I'll go tell my compadre that if we're gonna have all these Federales around all time, then we're gonna be in real bad shape. Really! Ya mean you don't believe me? I'm not afraid to speak my mind, and I swear by the mother who gave me life, that I'll go tell my compadre Demetrio . . ."

So he told him. Demetrio listened, very generously. And once Anastasio was done speaking, he replied:

"Compadre, what ya say is true. We're in a bad way: the soldiers grumble 'bout the promoted ones; the promoted ones, 'bout the officers; and the officers, 'bout us . . . And we're just about ready to tell Villa and Carranza to go off and play without us . . . But I figure that what's happening to us is the same thing as happened to that peasant in Tepatitlán. Remember? He never stopped complainin' about his boss, but he never stopped workin' neither. And tha's just how we are: we complain and complain, and then we kill and kill . . . But this isn't somethin' we should be sayin', compadre."

"Why not, compadre Demetrio?"

"Well, I don't know . . . 'Cause we just shouldn't . . . ya know? What ya should be doin' is getting' our people up. I've received orders to go back to stop a dispatch tha's supposed to go through Cuquío. In just a few days from now we'll have to go up against the damn Carranzistas for real, and this time we're gonna beat the hell out of 'em."

Valderrama—the vagabond of highways who one day joined the troop without anyone's knowing exactly when or where—caught some of Demetrio's words; and since even fools don't eat fire, he disappeared that same day as mysteriously as he had arrived.

V

They entered the streets of Juchipila just as the church bells were tolling, joyfully, loudly, with that particular tone that made the hearts of everyone from the surrounding canyons beat with emotion.

"Compadre, this reminds me of those times when the revolution was just startin', when we'd arrive in any small town and all the bells would ring loud for us, and all the people would come out to welcome us with music, with flags, and everyone would shout 'hurrah!' and even set off firecrackers," Anastasio Montañés said.

"Now they don't like us no more," Demetrio replied.

"Yes, since we're already 'beaten and routed,'" Quail remarked.

"It's not that . . . They can't stand the look of the others, either."

"But how are they supposed to like us, then, compadre?"

And they spoke no more of it.

They reached a plaza facing a coarse, massive octagonal church reminiscent of colonial times.

At one time the plaza must have been a garden, judging from the bare, mangy orange trees planted amid the remains of iron and wood benches.

The deep, joyful tolling of the church bells was heard again, followed by the harmonious voices of a female chorus rising with solemn melancholy from inside the church. The women of the town were singing the "Mysteries" to the accompanying chords of a bass guitar.

"What fiesta is being celebrated today, señora?" Venancio asked a little old lady who was rushing toward the church at full speed.

"The Sacred Heart of Jesus!" the pious woman replied, nearly choking.

They remembered that a year had passed already since they had taken Zacatecas, and they all became even sadder.[1]

Juchipila was in ruins, just like the other towns through which they had passed since Tepic, including Jalisco, Aguascalientes, and Zacatecas. The black traces of fire could be seen on roofless houses and burnt porticos. The remaining houses were boarded up. And occasionally a store would still be open, as if sarcastically, to show its empty shelves, which resembled the white skeletons of the horses scattered along every road. The awful mark of hunger could already be seen on the dirt-ridden faces of the people, in the bright flame of eyes that burned with fiery hatred whenever they beheld a passing soldier.

The soldiers wander the streets looking for food, but in vain; so they bite their tongues, burning with rage. The only eating house that is open immediately becomes full. They do not have any frijoles or tortillas: just chopped chilies and salt. The leaders show their pockets stuffed with bills; but they are useless, as are their threats.

"Pieces of paper, sure! Tha's what ya've brought us! Well, then go ahead and eat that!" says the owner, an insolent old woman with an enormous scar across her face, who adds, "I've already gotten in bed with death, so I'm certainly not scared to die now."

And in the sadness and desolation of the town, as the women sing in the church, the birds keep chirping in the foliage, and the song of the warblers is still heard from the dry branches of the orange trees.

VI

Beside herself with joy, holding her son's hand at her side, Demetrio Macías's wife runs up the path of the Sierra to meet her husband.

Absent for nearly two years![1]

They embrace but do not speak. She is overcome by sobs and tears.

An astounded Demetrio sees that his wife has aged, as if ten or twenty years had passed. Then he looked at the boy, who was staring at him with fright, and his heart skipped a beat when he saw a copy of his own steely facial lines in the boy's face, and of his own bright glare in the boy's eyes. He tried to reach out and hug him, but the child was very afraid and hid between his mother's legs.

"It's your father, son! It's your father!" But the boy, still fear-stricken, buried his head in the folds of his mother's skirts.

Demetrio, who had handed his horse off to an orderly, walked slowly next to his wife and son along the steep path of the Sierra.

"You're finally back, thank God that you've returned! Now you'll never leave us, right!? Say that you'll stay with us forever now!"

Demetrio's face clouded over.

An anguished silence grew between them.

A black cloud was rising behind the Sierra, and muffled thunder could be heard. Demetrio held back a sigh. Memories rushed upon him like bees to a beehive.

The rain started to fall in large drops, and they were forced to take refuge in a small rocky grotto.

The downpour erupted with a thundering sound, shaking all the white San Juan flowers, those bundles of stars found everywhere in the Sierra: hanging from the trees, on the boulders, amid the weeds, and between the pitahaya cacti.

Below, at the bottom of the canyon, through the veil of rain, could be seen straight, swaying palm trees, their angled tops rocking back and forth until a strong gust of wind blew their foliage open into green fans. And the Sierra was everywhere: sloping lines of hills and more hills, hills surrounded by mountains, which in turn were encircled by a wall of Sierra summits so tall that their blue tops were lost in the sapphire above.

"Demetrio, for God's sake! Don't leave again! My heart tells me that this time something's gonna happen to you!"

And once again she is overcome with sobs.

The frightened boy cries out loud, and she has to repress her own tremendous sorrow to console him.

The rain slowly ceases. A swallow with a silver underside and angled wings flies obliquely through the glass threads of rain, gleaming suddenly in the late afternoon sun.

"Why are you still fightin', Demetrio?"

Demetrio raises his eyebrows, absentmindedly picks up a small rock, and throws it toward the bottom of the canyon. Staring pensively down into the abyss, he says:

"Look at that rock, how nothin' can stop it now . . ."

VII

It was a truly glorious morning. After raining all night long, the sky had dawned covered with white clouds. Along the top ridge of the Sierra trotted wild colts, their manes standing on end and their tails sticking straight back, as proud as the peaks of the mountains raising their heads to kiss the clouds.

The soldiers marching along the steep, rocky terrain have caught the joy of the morning. No one thinks about the artful bullet that might be waiting for them further on. The great joy of setting out lies entirely in the unforeseen. And for this reason the soldiers are carefree, singing, laughing, talking. Their souls brim over with the soul of ancient nomadic tribes. Where they are going and whence they come matters not at all. Their only desire is to walk, to keep walking, and to never stop; to be the masters of the valley, of the plains, of the Sierra, of everything as far as the eye can see.

Trees, cacti, ferns: everything looks as if it has just been washed. The stones—with ocher like the rust of old armor—drip thick, transparent drops of water.

Macías's men are quiet for a moment. Apparently they have heard a familiar noise: a weapon fired in the distance. But several minutes pass and nothing more is heard.

"In this same Sierra," Demetrio says, "I, with only twenty men, took out more than five hundred Federales."

As Demetrio begins to recount that famous military deed, his men realize the grave danger in which they now find themselves. What if the enemy, instead of still being two days away, is actually hiding in the tall weeds of the ravine around them, along the bottom of which they are currently marching? But who among them would dare show his fear? When had Demetrio's men ever said: "No, we won't go that way"?

When distant firing begins, up ahead where the vanguard is, no one is even that surprised. The recruits turn on their heels in an unbridled retreat, seeking some way out of the canyon.

A curse escapes from Demetrio's dry throat:

"Fire! Shoot anyone who runs away!"

"Let's take the heights from them!" he then roars, like a wild animal.

But the enemy, hiding by the thousands, unleashes its machine guns, and Demetrio's men fall like ears of corn cut by a sickle.[1]

Demetrio sheds tears of rage and pain when Anastasio slides slowly off his horse, without as much as a sigh, to lie outstretched, motionless. Venancio falls beside him, his chest horribly ripped open by the machine gun, and the Indian goes off the edge of the precipice and rolls to the bottom of the abyss. All of a sudden Demetrio finds himself alone. The bullets whiz by his ears like a hailstorm. He dismounts, drags himself along the rocks until he finds cover, places a stone to protect his head, and—with his chest set against the ground—begins to fire.

The enemy spreads out, chasing the rare fugitives still left amid the chaparral.

Demetrio aims and hits every time . . . Bang! Bang! Bang!

His famous marksmanship fills him with joy. He hits everywhere he sets his eye. He goes through one magazine and loads another into his rifle. And he aims again . . .

The smoke from the firing guns does not dissipate. The cicadas intone their mysterious, imperturbable song; the doves sing softly in the nooks between the rocks; the cows graze peacefully.

The Sierra is dressed in gala. Above its inaccessible peaks, a pure white fog descends like a snowy veil on a bride's head.

At the foot of a craggy hollow—enormous and magnificent as the portico of an old cathedral—Demetrio Macías, his eyes fixed forever, continues to aim with the barrel of his rifle . . .

Notes

INTRODUCTION

1. See Chronology of the Mexican Revolution (p. xxi).
2. Julián Medina is mentioned in part I, chapter II.
3. See Chronology of Mariano Azuela's Life and Work (p. xxv).
4. For a thorough critical study of the evolution of Azuela's *Los de abajo,* see Stanley L. Robe's *Azuela and the Mexican Underdogs.*
5. *Modernismo* was a Spanish-American literary movement that lasted from approximately 1880 to 1910. Although styles differed from writer to writer, *Modernista* writers believed in and practiced an aesthetic and a cult of beauty; emulated the French symbolist, Parnassian, and decadent poets; and often made references to exotic lands. The most important *Modernista* writers were the Nicaraguan Rubén Darío and the Cuban José Martí. Mexico also had two leading *Modernista* writers—Manuel Gutiérrez Nájera and Amado Nervo—with whose work Azuela would certainly have been familiar.

PART 1

I

1. **Palomo:** Demetrio Macías's and his wife's dog is named Palomo, Spanish for a kind of dove or pigeon. The dog's name is relevant in several of the first few scenes.
2. **Federales:** The common term for the Mexican regular or federal army, especially during the three decades of authoritarian rule by Porfirio Díaz (1876–80; 1884–1911). During the revolution, the Federales were the government troops who fought against the revolutionaries—first under Díaz (through 1911) and then under Victoriano Huerta (1913–14).

3. **"I'll turn your house into a dovecote":** In Spanish, the Federale tells Demetrio's wife that he will turn her house into a *palomar* (dovecote). This is a play on words, since the Federales have just killed her dog, Palomo.

4. **Escobedo:** Small town in the state of Coahuila.

5. **Jalpa:** Town in the state of Zacatecas.

II

1. **Moyahua:** Town in the state of Zacatecas.

2. **pitahaya cacti:** Tall cacti that bear edible fruit, native to the southwestern United States and northern Mexico.

3. **Hostotipaquillo:** Small town in the state of Jalisco.

4. **Julián Medina:** Reference to the leader—who became one of Villa's generals—of a revolutionary band with which Azuela traveled as medical officer from October 1914 through April 1915.

5. **metate:** A flat or partly hollowed, usually oblong stone on which grains, such as corn, are ground by means of a smaller stone.

6. Quail's name in the Spanish original is Codorniz. See Introduction, p. xvi for a discussion of the translation of most of the characters' nicknames.

7. Lard's name in the Spanish original is el Manteca.

8. **huisache trees:** A thorny, shrubby acacia found in the southern United States and throughout Mexico and Central America.

9. **thirty-thirty:** Nickname given by the rebels during Mexico's revolution for their carbines; refers to the Winchester 30-30 carbine. There is even a famous *corrido* (Mexican ballad) of that name from the time, entitled "Carabina 30-30."

III

1. The Indian's name in the Spanish original is Meco.

2. **vara:** A Spanish measure varying in length in different localities, usually about thirty-three inches.

IV

1. **Juchipila:** Town in the state of Zacatecas.

2. *The Wandering Jew:* 1844 novel by the French author Eugène Sue (1804–57). *The Sun of May* (*El sol de mayo*): 1868 novel

by Juan A. Mateos (1831–1913), one of the most popular Mexican writers of the second half of the nineteenth century. The novel has not been translated into English.

3. *jícara*: The Spanish name, used in Mexico and Central America, for the calabash tree or its fruit, the calabash gourd.

V

1. *curro*: Derogatory term denoting a city slicker who in turn looks pretentiously down on the poor. See Introduction, p. xvi for a discussion of the translation of most of the characters' nicknames and why *curro* is left in Spanish.

2. **"Carranzo"**: Luis Cervantes probably says "Carranza," not "Carranzo," but Anastasio in all likelihood misunderstands, unaware of who this key political figure is, or why Cervantes would identify himself as being on the side of Carranza. At this stage in the revolution (in mid-1913, near the start of the novel), Venustiano Carranza (1859–1920), the governor of the state of Coahuila and an elder of the revolution, was considered the commander in chief of the revolutionary forces against General Victoriano Huerta's federation forces. It is reasonable, then, that Cervantes would call out the name Carranza hoping that the group of revolutionaries would respond favorably.

VI

1. **Most Holy Mother of Guadalupe:** A sixteenth-century Mexican icon of the Virgin Mary, said to have appeared to Juan Diego Cuauhtlatoatzin on the hill of Tepeyac near Mexico City from December 9 through December 12, 1531. The Virgin of Guadalupe is Mexico's most famous religious and cultural image. A key element of the Virgin of Guadalupe's uniqueness and importance is that she is a mestiza Virgin, and thus representative of Latin American mestizo culture and Mexican identity in particular.

2. **Villa:** Francisco "Pancho" Villa (1878–1923). The foremost leader of the Mexican Revolution in the northern area of Mexico, especially in the state of Chihuahua, where Villa was provisional governor in 1913 and 1914. Often referred to as *El centauro del norte* (the centaur of the north) because of his celebrated cavalry attacks as a general, Villa organized an army of twenty thousand men during the height of the revolution.

Most of these soldiers were vaqueros and peasants, and Villa's own humble origins contributed to what would become his legendary fame.

3. **"We get lousy paper money"**: Reference to the issue of the different denominations of money with which soldiers—both Federales and revolutionaries—were paid during the Mexican Revolution. "That murderer" refers to Victoriano Huerta and the (probably accurate) rumors circulating during the revolution that he ordered the assassination of Francisco Madero in February 1913.

VIII

1. **"before long she was addressing him informally"**: In the Spanish original, Camila begins to address Luis Cervantes in the informal *tú* instead of the formal *usted*.

2. **the federation**: refers to the official government of Mexico, consolidated under the authoritarian presidencies of Porfirio Díaz until the revolution, and then reinstated during Victoriano Huerta's dictatorship, 1914–15. The reference to Huerta's friends and family fleeing Mexico City, which preceded Huerta's own exile from Mexico, places the action of the novel at this point right around July 1914, at the fall of Huerta's dictatorship.

IX

1. **nixtamal**: Blue corn ground by hand—usually with a metate (see chap. II, n. 5)—to make tortillas.

2. **"Well, María Antonia has got her the 'curse'"**: As part of their gossip, the women here are saying that another character, María Antonia, is currently having her menstrual period (the euphemism they use for this is "the curse"), from which she apparently suffers cramps (which they refer to as "the colic").

3. **palomo**: In the Spanish original, the small pigeon is a *palomo,* which is meant to resonate with the beginning of the novel and the name of Demetrio's dog.

X

1. **Spanish flies**: Dried beetles formerly considered an aphrodisiac.

XI

1. **madroño:** A small, attractive evergreen tree with dark, lustrous green leaves, red berries, and hard wood.
2. **"La Adelita":** The most famous *corrido* [ballad] of the Mexican Revolution. Intimately associated with the revolution and sung especially by the Villistas, the song tells the story of a soldier in love with a girl named Adelita. "La Adelita" was almost as much a defining image as the sombreros worn by the revolutionaries.
3. **atole:** A kind of corn or other meal, or gruel or porridge made of this.

XII

1. **aguardiente:** A very strong distilled liquor, such as brandy or pulque, usually made from the sap of the agave or maguey.
2. **"The Federales had fortified El Grillo and La Bufa":** The news that Demetrio Macías and his men hear corresponds to the historical moment right before the revolutionaries attacked and took Zacatecas, capital of the state of Zacatecas. At this point in the novel, the federal armies, under Huerta's leadership, are preparing to defend Zacatecas, while the revolutionaries, under the leadership of Villa and including Villa's general Pánfilo Natera, are preparing to attack the city. El Grillo and La Bufa are summits overlooking the city; the fighting over these was central to the outcome of the battle. The battle itself (*Toma de Zacatecas* [taking of Zacatecas]), in June 1914, was one of the bloodiest of the Mexican Revolution and the turning point that would lead to Huerta's defeat.
3. **Pánfilo Natera (1882–1951):** A veridical revolutionary leader who would become one of Villa's generals. Interestingly, Natera is the only historical figure who actually appears as a character in the novel; the other major ones (Villa, Huerta, Carranza, etc.) are referred and alluded to many times but do not actually make an appearance per se.

XIII

1. **"the one about how they killed Señor Madero":** Macías is referring to the assassinations of Madero and his vice president

(Pino Suárez), but is confusing several key names here. In what was known as *La decena trágica* (the ten tragic days), in February 1913, Huerta usurped power from Madero in a military coup and in all likelihood ordered Madero and Suárez killed. Félix Díaz was the nephew of Porfirio Díaz and an old political crony from the *Porfiriato* period with whom Huerta conspired as part of his coup.

Macías's confusion raises the issue of his motivations for fighting, and the extent that they are personal rather than ideological, as revealed by his ignorance of and distance from the main political events of the revolution during this time. Macías himself speaks to how he became a revolutionary in the first place in the account he tells Cervantes at this moment of the novel.

2. **"Sayin' that I was a Maderista"**: A supporter of Francisco Madero (1873–1913), the wealthy landowner who started the revolution against Porfirio Díaz in November 1910, and became president of Mexico, 1911–13. Promising land and agrarian reform, he had broad popular support at first. He was arrested and then assassinated when Victoriano Huerta seized power in February 1913.

3. **"I was about to rise up and join the revolution"**: From Macías's account of his "run-in" with Don Mónico, and in particular from this reference to Madero, we can deduce that this occurred during Madero's presidency, between May 1911 and February 1913.

4. **"And once it is over, they will say to you"**: Cervantes is referring to the fact that after Madero came to power, following his successful overthrow of Porfirio Díaz's regime, he did not deliver on his promises of land and agrarian reform, which led to a quick rift with leaders such as Zapata in the south and Villa in the north.

5. **"That is what Villa, Natera, and Carranza are fighting for"**: At this stage of the revolution—and of the novel—in 1913, Villa is still aligned with Carranza. Natera, one of Villa's generals, will remain loyal to Villa throughout the revolution; Villa and Carranza will begin fighting each other in late 1914.

XV

1. **mezcal**: A strong alcoholic spirit distilled from the fermented sap of the agave cactus; similar to tequila or pulque.

2. **General Álvaro Obregón (1880–1928):** At first, an important supporter of Madero's revolt against and overthrow of Porfirio Díaz. Then, when Huerta overthrows Madero (in 1913), Obregón joins forces with Carranza to eventually help defeat Huerta in July 1914. After that, as Carranza's minister of war, Obregón fights against Villa's armies in 1915.

3. **Owl:** Owl's name in the Spanish original is Tecolote.

XVI

1. **"he would invariably recall the deeds at the Ciudadela":** A historical reference to Huerta's overthrow of Madero in 1913, which led to Madero's murder and Huerta's proclaiming himself provisional president of Mexico. Huerta would stay in power from 1913 to 1914, establishing a harsh military dictatorship. The Federale captain in the novel is here fondly remembering his participation as a cadet in the coup (on Huerta's side).

    The Ciudadela (the Citadel) was the main military headquarters for federal troops in Mexico City at the time.

2. **General Aureliano Blanquet (1849–1919):** A military officer from the time of Porfirio Díaz, in 1913—during the overthrow led by Huerta—he is the one who apprehends Madero. Huerta then promotes him to division general and then minister of war and the navy, a post Blanquet holds from 1913 to 1914.

3. **"Long live His Honor General Don Victoriano Huerta":** From this imagined letter (which the Federale officer drafts in his mind), and the officer's evocation of Huerta, it is evident that the actions in this section of the novel are set while Huerta is still in power, between February 1913 and July 1914.

XVIII

1. **"the same day that Pánfilo Natera was commencing his advance":** This battle, on June 23, 1914, known as the *Toma de Zacatecas* (taking of Zacatecas) between the federal armies of Victoriano Huerta and the Constitutionalist troops of General Francisco Villa, was one of the bloodiest of the Mexican Revolution. Villa's victory would lead to the end of the Huerta regime.

2. **Tepic:** Capital city of the state of Nayarit. **Durango:** Capital city of the state of Durango.

3. **"the time of Madero"**: Solís is referring to the period when Francisco Madero was president, from November 1911 (shortly after his successful revolt against Porfirio Díaz) to February 1913 (when Huerta overthrows Madero).

4. *El Regional*: Both *El Regional* and *El País* are veridical newspapers that were published during and covered the Mexican Revolution.

5. **northern division**: A reference to Francisco Villa and his legendary army.

XIX

1. **weight of his "advance"**: The revolutionaries in Demetrio Macías's group refer to what they have gathered—ostensibly their loot—as an "advance," as a way to say that this is what they deserve to be paid (in lieu of any formal payment) for their service.

XX

1. **"Mexican Napoleon"**: One of the nicknames attributed to Villa; the most famous of these was "The Centaur of the North."

2. **"Oh, Villa! The battles of Ciudad Juárez"**: Natera's men are telling stories from some of Villa's most famous and spectacular victories. In particular:

> The Battle of Ciudad Juárez (April–May 1911)—in which Pascual Orozco and Francisco Villa defeat the Federale army—a battle crucial to Madero's overthrow of the Díaz regime.
>
> The Battle of Tierra Blanca (November 19, 1913), one of Villa's legendary successes, in which he defeats General José Inés Salvador in Tierra Blanca (in the state of Zacatecas).
>
> The Battle of Torreón: (October 2, 1913), when Villa's division of the north captures Torreón (in the state of Coahuila), and Villa becomes a civil governor for the first time.
>
> The Battle of Chihuahua (December 8, 1913), in which the city of Chihuahua falls to Villa and his army (the northern division).

3. **Villa's aeroplanes:** The Mexican Revolution was the first war in which airplanes played a decisive military role. Although in this section of the novel it is Villa's use of airplanes that is evoked with passion and glory, the use of airplanes would actually be a decisive factor in Huerta's defeat of Villa, beginning in 1915.

XXI

1. **"The machine guns did all the work":** First reference in the novel to the use of machine guns by the federal army. In the Mexican Revolution, Álvaro Obregón would use these successfully to defeat Villa in several key battles in 1915, including the Battle of Celaya in April.
2. **"to defeat a wretched assassin":** Solís could be referring to the original revolutionary uprisings against the dictator Porfirio Díaz, or to the revolt (led by Villa and others) over Victoriano Huerta, who is said to have had Madero assassinated in February 1913.

PART 2

I

1. *chorro:* A vaquero; a Mexican cowboy.
2. Towhead Margarito's name in the Spanish original is el güero Margarito.
3. War Paint's name in the Spanish original is Pintada.
4. **Torreón:** City in the state of Coahuila. Torreón was taken by the Maderista forces on May 15, 1911, and then by the Villista forces on October 1, 1913. Torreón would also be taken and sacked by Villa in 1916.
5. **Hidalgo del Parral:** Town in the state of Coahuila. On March 24, 1912, Villa takes this town. This is also the town in which Villa would be assassinated, on July 20, 1923.
6. **"'cause he slipped two bills from Huerta":** Another reference to the various bills printed during the revolution (see part 1 chap. VI, n. 3).
7. **Chihuahua:** The capital of the state of Chihuahua.
8. **Seven Sisters:** A colloquial expression for the Pleiades.

III

1. **menudo:** A thick, spicy soup traditionally made with tripe, calf's feet, and hominy.
2. **Tierra Blanca:** Small town in the state of Chihuahua.

V

1. **Antonio Plaza (1833–82):** Poet and journalist from the state of Guanajuato, Plaza studied law in Mexico City. He wrote impassioned journalistic pieces defending liberal ideas, and very sentimental Romantic poetry. His work has not been translated into English.
2. **"and a few bills, of the kind issued by Huerta":** Another reference to the different currencies printed during the revolution. The women in Don Mónico's house have but a few of the "Huerta bills"—i.e., from the time of Huerta's presidency (1913–14)—which would have lost essentially all their value by July 1914, when Huerta went into exile.

VIII

1. **Orozquistas:** The followers of Pascual Orozco (1882–1915). Orozco supported Madero in the overthrow of Porfirio Díaz, and in the early stages of the revolution, after a series of victories over the federation, he was a hero in the north, especially in the state of Chihuahua (in particular, on May 10, 1911, when Orozco and Villa seized Ciudad Juárez). However, Orozco eventually has a falling-out with Madero and revolts against him. But Orozco's revolt is unsuccessful, as Madero has Victoriano Huerta put it down (in 1912, before Huerta turns on Madero, to seize control of the federation himself). Orozco is forced into exile in the United States; from there, he eventually recognizes Huerta's presidency and, as the commanding general of all Mexican Federal forces, leads attacks against the revolutionaries and Pancho Villa. During this stage of the fighting, after Villa takes Zacatecas (in 1914), Huerta resigns and Orozco flees into exile again (along with Huerta). This leaves a number of "Orozquistas" for Villa's supporters to go after, which is what Macías has just been ordered to do in the novel.

2. The Indian confuses Orozco with Huerta. He is apparently thinking of the events of February 1913, which led to the assassination of Madero a few days after Huerta, the commander of the armed forces, conspired with Félix Díaz (Porfirio Díaz's nephew), Bernardo Reyes, and U.S. Ambassador Henry Lane Wilson, against Madero, which culminated in the ten days known as *La decena tragica* [the tragic ten days]. Huerta took over the presidency on February 18, 1913, and Francisco Madero was shot four days later.

Meanwhile, Towhead Margarito apparently once met someone also named Pascual Orozco, just like the famous general from the revolution. The Indian's confusion—and Margarito's comical doubling of names—once again reveal the extent to which Macías and his men remain very distant from the major political events of the time.

XI

1. **Tepatitlán de Morelos:** Town in the state of Jalisco.
2. **Cuquío:** Small town in the state of Jalisco.
3. **Aguascalientes:** Capital of the state of Aguascalientes.
4. **four crisp, brand-new two-faced bills:** Once again, a reference to the various bills printed during the revolution, in this case, the bills known as *billetes dos caritas* (two-faced bills) that Villa had printed during his brief period as governor of the state of Chihuahua in 1914–15.

XII

1. **Lagos de Moreno:** City in the state of Jalisco, Lagos is where the author was born.

XIII

1. **"To cast your vote, General, for the provisional president":** As a revolutionary leader, Demetrio Macías has been invited to the Convención de Aguascalientes (Convention of Aguascalientes), held in November 1914, at which the revolutionary leaders (who had just defeated Huerta) met in an attempt to reconcile their differences and plan for the future. This effort would fail, however, and a rift would develop between

Villa and Zapata on one side, and Carranza and Obregón on the other.

XIV

1. **Silao:** City in the state of Guanajuato.
2. **Irapuato:** City in the state of Guanajuato.
3. **"Now it's Villa against Carranza":** Natera is informing Macías that the Convention of Aguascalientes has failed, and part of the resulting rifts is that Carranza and Villa will now begin to fight against each other, in what would in essence be a civil war.
4. **"the convention won't recognize Carranza":** When the discussions at the Convention of Aguascalientes of November 1914 break down, Carranza is deposed and a provisional president (Eulalio Gutiérrez) is installed. After this, Villa (in the north), as well as Zapata in the south, now fights a civil war against Carranza. Soon thereafter, Carranza and Obregón will flee to Veracruz, and Villa and Zapata will occupy Mexico City. However, the urban centers continued to be powerhouses of constitutionalist support for Carranza, and Villa's actions in the capital soon force him to leave in 1915. Constitutionalist (i.e., Carranza's) forces will continue to hound him until he is defeated in battle in April 1915.
5. **"So on which side are you going to fight?":** After explaining the political fallout of the Convention of Aguascalientes, Natera asks Macías if he will side with Carranza or with Villa. Macías apparently does not know or does not care about the political details, and seems unable to make an informed decision. Macías chooses to remain loyal to Natera, who earlier made him a general, and thus in turn remains a Villista (since Natera will keep fighting on Villa's side).

PART 3

I

1. **"El Paso, Texas, May 16, 1915":** As is evident from this letter's date and setting, Luis Cervantes's "move" to El Paso neatly parallels the move that Mariano Azuela made after Villa was defeated by Carranza and his troops in 1915.

2. **"Didn't we already defeat the federation?"**: Anastasio Montañés is expressing his frustration over the fighting between the various revolutionary factions well into 1920, even though "the federation" had already been defeated (Porifirio Díaz's federation was defeated in 1911; Victoriano Huerta's federation was defeated in 1914).

3. **"Os ex ossibus meis et caro de carne mea"**: In Latin in the original, Valderrama is quoting from the Bible, Genesis 2:23. In English, this verse is usually rendered as "This is now bone of my bone and flesh of my flesh."

II

1. **Durango:** Capital of the state of Durango.

2. **Carranzista scorpions:** In the Spanish original, the term for "Carranzista scorpions" is *carranclanes,* a pejorative way of referring to Carranza supporters during this period of the revolution. The term is a neologism combining "Carranzistas" with "alacranes" (scorpions).

3. **Celaya:** City in the state of Guanajuato, and also a reference to Villa's defeat to Huerta in the Battle of Celaya in April, 1915.

4. **General Tomás Urbina:** Known as "El león de Durango" (The Lion of Durango), a Villista leader who tended to evoke more fear than admiration. Later in the revolution, in September 1915, Urbina would desert Villa and devote himself primarily to banditry.

5. **Villa's tremendous defeat in Celaya:** Refers to Villa's defeat in the Battle of Celaya (April 6–15, 1915), at the hand of the constitutionalist troops, led by General Álvaro Obregón. Obregón lost one of his arms in the fighting, but defeated Villa's army. This battle was the beginning of Villa's decline.

IV

1. **"The trail of blood of the first revolutionaries of 1910:** Valderrama is evoking the memory of the first revolutionaries who challenged the regime of Porfirio Díaz in 1910.

2. **"Juchipila, crib of the Revolution of 1910":** Still evoking the memory of the first revolutionaries, Valderrama in particular associates Juchipila (in the state of Zacatecas) as the birthplace of the revolution.

V

1. **a year had passed already since they had taken Zacatecas:** This reference further establishes the date of the current actions of the novel, since the taking of Zacatecas occurred on June 1914.

VI

1. **Absent for nearly two years!:** This line, combined with the date of Luis Cervantes's letter from El Paso at the beginning of part 3, and the reference to how much time has passed since the taking of Zacatecas, allows us to establish that the entire novel covers a span of two years (1913–15). This also allows us to insert and better understand the actions of Demetrio Macías and his men within the historical context of the Mexican Revolution.

VII

1. **unleashes its machine guns, and Demetrio's men fall:** This, the final battle of the novel, resonates with the manner in which Obregón was able to defeat Villa (as of April 1915)—through the military innovation, which Obregón imported from Germany, of using machine guns against cavalry charges. From a historical point of view, the novel thus ends as Villa is about to suffer a series of defeats, as Obregón would persevere with this new use of machine guns, a military strategy that proved to overcome the courage of large numbers of Villa's northern division.